Mating Fever

Morgan Clan Bears
Book 3

By
Theresa Hissong

Disclaimer:
This book is a work of fiction. Any resemblance to any person, living or dead is purely coincidental. The names of people, places, and/or things are all created from the author's mind and are only used for entertainment.

Due to the content, this book is recommended for adults 18 years and older.

©2020 Theresa Hissong
All Rights Reserved

Cover Design:
Gray Publishing Services

Editing by:
Heidi Ryan
Amour the Line Editing

Follow Theresa at
Authortheresahissong.com
Or
www.facebook.com/authortheresahissong

Dedication:

To the readers:
May we all meet again.

Contents:
Prologue
Chapter 1
Chapter 2
Chapter 3
Chapter 4
Chapter 5
Chapter 6
Chapter 7
Chapter 8
Chapter 9
Chapter 10
Chapter 11
Chapter 12
Chapter 13
Chapter 14
Chapter 15
Chapter 16
Chapter 17
Chapter 18
Chapter 19
Epilogue
About the Author

Prologue

Gaia started the coffee brewing five minutes before the diner opened for the breakfast rush. With the oncoming spring, the people of town were more active. The snowfall she'd given them early in the year had been received with excitement by the little children. It didn't matter that the adults were agitated with the aftermath, because Gaia was in a great mood and wanted to give back to the youth.

New laws had been made over taking care of her earthly home. New foundations and organizations undertaking the massive amount of waste in the oceans had been announced at the beginning of the year, and that made her beam with pride. The younger generation was finally doing something to restore the Earth's natural state. It would take many years to undo the sins of the past, but at least the humans were on track.

"Are you ready?" she asked Tony, her cook, as he prepared his station for the morning rush. She was in a great mood and wanted to pay it forward.

Several human males were already in the parking lot. It was five in the morning on a Sunday, and from the looks of it, they were on their way to a local lake to do some fishing. She smiled as they entered, making a note to keep the air warm and the sun bright over the water to aide in giving them a little luck.

"Morning, Gaia!" Several of the men were regulars, and she already knew what they wanted the moment they sat down. She poured several cups of black coffee and added three creamers for one of the men.

"Here you go," she said as she placed the cups. "Everyone want their regular?"

A round of agreements sent her to the kitchen window to inform Tony they were ready to eat. More customers entered as her new waitress, Mara Wood, arrived a few minutes late. Gaia gave her a scowl, but otherwise left her alone. The poor human was living with a terrible mate, and she knew he'd been the one to hold her up that morning. He was also responsible for the bruises she kept hidden under long-sleeved shirts and a lot of makeup.

He would get his one day.

After the group of males left to start their fishing trip, Gaia waited on the three humans sitting at her counter. "Can I have a blueberry muffin?" a voice she already knew rumbled out behind her.

With a heavy sigh, she turned around to find the local sheriff and angel, Garrett Lynch, sitting where Mr. Williams had been only moments before. She scooped up the other man's payment and entered it into the register, wiping her hands on the apron she wore.

She hadn't seen much of the angel lately, and after their little run in last spring at her home, he'd pretty much left her alone. "What else can I get you, Sheriff?"

He waited until she retrieved the muffin from the bakery case to clasp his hands on top of the table. "I need to speak to you privately."

"I'm sure you can see I'm quite busy right now, Garrett," she hedged. With Mara there, she really didn't need to rush around as much, but she used the excuse anyway. The last time they had been alone together, some semi-serious flirting had gone down, and she wasn't sure how to take it.

"It's about your…boys," he said, lowering his voice.

The mention of the Morgan bears sent a chill up her spine. The sheriff had no business with them, and he best keep his nose out of their daily lives. She narrowed her eyes and leaned over the counter, so her mouth was close to his ear. "Those boys are mine, and you best keep them out of your mouth."

"What I have to say involves your bears," he replied with a whisper.

Her eyes swirled like the eye of a hurricane as the anger over speaking their species out loud in a room full of humans brought out her darker side. The grizzlies were the only ones not known to the humans, and they wanted to keep it that way. "Go to my office."

The sheriff stood and placed a few bills on the counter for his uneaten muffin before he strode to the back of the diner. Whatever the lawman had to say better be worth him almost exposing the grizzlies to the humans.

"Mara, can you watch the counter?" Gaia asked her waitress as she removed her apron. "I'll be back shortly." The meeting with the sheriff wouldn't take long.

She pushed open the door to her office a little too hard, making the male turn around to see what the noise was all about. He frowned at her, but Gaia didn't comment. She wanted to get down to business and tell the angel to leave her diner.

"What is this all about?" she barked, folding her arms across her chest.

"It's about the clan," he sighed, his tall, tight body deflating just a bit. From the exhausted look on his face, Gaia realized what he had to say must be important.

"What about them?" she pressed.

"The humans know," he began, pulling a chair away from the front of her desk to take a seat. "They know about the grizzlies, and I had a vision that a group of four hunters are coming for them today."

"Well," she chuckled. "That's not going to be a problem. They've been in hibernation and will be for another week or two. There is no way they'll get to the clan. They're in their dens." The bears didn't like to leave their homes until a week or two after the spring equinox.

"I don't care what they usually do," he barked. "I've seen it happen, and my visions are always correct."

"I thought you were in charge of the werepanthers?" she asked, wondering why he was even talking about her bears. She oversaw them...not the sheriff.

"I am, but the vision was given to me by the gods," he replied, glancing toward the ceiling. Gaia rolled her eyes. Their gods were always stirring the pot down on her planet, and she really wished they'd back off. "I saw it, Gaia."

"What did you see?" she asked, ignoring the desire to claw his eyes out for stepping into her territory.

"Gunnar and his destined mate will be shot today," he admitted. The sheriff approached her, cupping her upper arms. An electric pulse shivered through her when his eyes flashed white. "Please send word to them."

"Are you sure about this?" she gasped, feeling her heart thunder in her human body.

"I don't question the visions they allow me," he replied. His radio crackled with a call from dispatch, but he reached back and lowered the volume on the unit that was clipped to his belt. "I was sent here to care for the panthers. I'm only allowed to see if anything human is coming for them. With the recent work of other shifters in the area, I've been blind. When this vision hit me this morning, I was confused, but I also knew not to discredit it. I came to you as soon as I could. Whatever you do with the information is on you, but I would at least contact one of those Morgan brothers to let them know. I already tried to call them, but they didn't answer."

"They don't use their phones during their hibernation," she admitted. "They might wake up a few times and check their messages, but it's not often."

"Please, just call them," he urged, dropping his hands. "I'm not going out to their land, because I am not welcome. I figured it was quicker to get the message to you than to drive out to their land, anyway."

"I can reach them," she replied, rubbing her temples. "I'll go now."

"Good," he nodded. "Thanks for the muffin."

The sheriff left her standing in the middle of the room. With a white flash, he was gone, and she was left with the information. Humans were on the hunt for her bears, and she'd move the heavens to make sure Gunnar and his soon-to-be mate were out of harm's way.

As she dialed the male's phone number, a rumble of thunder sounded outside. Her eyes swirled faster as the call was left unanswered. She would drive those humans away from the clan, and she'd rain hellfire down on them if they laid one finger on her bears.

Chapter 1

Gunnar Morgan stretched as he woke from hibernation. His bear rumbled at the scent of Anna Claire still sleeping in his bedroom. Once winter came, she had been living in the one temporary home on the property, but she was scared to be there alone. Gunnar had offered to move her into his room and place a spare bed out in his living quarters so they could be together during the winter. She'd agreed, and that had made his heart swell.

They'd forged a friendship over the summer and fall, but they hadn't touched. Anna Claire was still struggling with her demons when they had bedded down for the winter, and he didn't know if she would ever be ready for a mating. His beast was fighting him every second of the day to touch her and show her how much they wanted to be her mate.

"Gunnar?" Anna Claire's sleep-fogged voice called out.

"I'm here," he promised as he pushed the bedroom door open. His bear rumbled in his mind when he saw her nestled in a mound of blankets and several pillows. She'd made a nest in the center of her bed for her winter slumber. "Are you ready for spring?"

"I am," she whispered, but her eyes betrayed her. She cast a glance at her lap, and a soft sigh fell from her pouty lips. "I think I am."

"You can wake up whenever you'd like," he reassured her. Gods, if he could kill her father again, he would. The male had allowed men to touch her and pass her around like her life was worth nothing. Last spring, they'd found her trussed up in the forest with a gash across her abdomen and thighs He'd vowed to himself he'd see her healed from the trauma.

"Can you give me a minute?" she asked, a soft blush painting her cheeks.

"I'm going to make some coffee out here in the kitchen," he advised. "We don't have to go into the main house for a few more days."

"What day is it anyway?" she asked.

"It's March nineteenth," he answered, looking at his watch. "We usually don't gather with the others until about three days after the first day of spring." Bears were groggy coming out of hibernation, and they were hungry. The Morgan bears usually spent those three days eating as much as they could to bulk up from the long winter sleep.

"That's good," she nodded, relief making her body sag.

"You can sleep," he urged. "I'm going to start making some food, too. If you are feeling up to eating, it'll be ready in about an hour."

"That sounds amazing," she hummed as she rubbed her flat stomach. "I could eat a whole cow."

"Supplies are low, but I have just the thing." He winked and turned from the room, closing the door to give her some privacy.

At least Anna Claire was talking and acting the same as she'd done right before the winter solstice. He'd worked hard to keep the lines of communication open with her, letting the female know he was going to be patient with her. The last thing he wanted to do was give her any reason to think he would force a mating with her.

He and Anna Claire already knew they were mates. Their bears had already claimed each other by scent, but not by blood or touch. He'd seen what had been done to the female, and he wouldn't blame her if she never wanted to have a mate. He'd be her friend and protector for the rest of her natural life if she made the decision to stay unmated.

Gunnar whipped up a high protein meal and left it in the oven to cook. He set a timer and made his way out to the main house to check on supplies. They'd stocked their quarters with food before the hibernation but left the bulk of things in the main house. Since he was awake, he might as well make a list of things they'd need for the next few months until Ada could prepare their garden.

He was thankful the female had taken over the patch of land behind the house. Gunnar had been in charge of that when he was younger, before his parents were killed, but let it go when they were thrust into the farming business left to them by their father. Ada had grown enough vegetables for them to last through the winter, and Gunnar and Anna Claire had spent many afternoons bonding over canning the foods to give them a longer shelf life. When he reached the living room, he saw his brother, Rex, in the kitchen grabbing one of two bags of potatoes.

"Hey, brother," Rex boomed. His mate had given birth to a male cub during the winter, and he'd been pampering her all throughout their hibernation. "How's Anna Claire?"

"She's as well as to be expected." Gunnar paused to frown. "She struggled the first few weeks of hibernation, but eventually settled."

"Maybe things will change once we get moving again." Rex shrugged, but his face had still fallen at the mention of the female.

"How's Ada? Thane?" Gunnar inquired. He'd only seen the cub a few times over the winter. Just because they were hibernating didn't mean they slept the entire winter away. They would emerge every couple of weeks to check on their home and grab supplies if they were needed. Very rarely did they ever leave the homestead.

"Perfect," Rex blushed. "They're perfect."

"Have you heard from Drake or Tessa?"

"They're awake, but you know Drake." Rex

rolled his eyes. "He's going to stay locked up with his mate and cub until the last day."

Gunnar laughed and reached into the pantry to grab a can of coffee for Anna Claire. They hadn't stocked any before winter.

"I'm planning on making a run to the fields tomorrow. Do you want to ride along?" Rex asked.

"Yeah," Gunnar said with a nod. "I'm going to check on the elders and the O'Kelly boys sometime later today."

"Ada talked to Martha two weeks ago, and they were doing very well in their cabins," Rex informed him. "It's odd, but nice having them here."

"It's new for us, but I'm grateful for Luca and Ransom's help this season," Gunnar admitted, picking up the last bag of potatoes. "Let me know when you want to leave, and I'll ride with you."

"You'll call me if the elders are in need of anything?" Rex added a bag of sugar to his stack of supplies once Gunnar had moved away from the pantry.

"Sure will."

Rex gave him a nod and disappeared down the hallway leading to his quarters. He could hear their cub fussing a little, but the sound was cut off when Rex closed the door.

As he closed the cabinet doors, Gunnar felt a craving deep in the pit of his stomach. His beast stirred, moving just underneath his skin. He felt his canines thicken in his mouth. Clamping down on the realization, he tried to push at his beast. Mating season was upon them, and as hard as he tried, he couldn't resist the pull toward the quarters he shared with the woman who wasn't ready to come out of her shell from her attacks to touch him.

Gunnar, her possible mate, had left the quarters to grab some supplies. Anna Claire took that opportunity to shower and grab some new clothes. She used the hairdryer under his sink to dry her long, blonde hair. She styled it simply and put on a pair of jeans and a thick sweater that fit her small body.

As she entered the living quarters, she found Gunnar in the small kitchen, removing a dish from the oven. She hummed at the scent of chicken and potatoes. "That smells amazing."

She'd lost a lot of weight over the winter, but that was normal for bears. The weight would return in the next few weeks as they all prepared themselves for spring. The males had work to do to plant the crops, and the females would take over on the homestead.

Ada had already planned out their backyard garden for the summer, and Anna Claire couldn't wait to get started.

She finally had something of her own, and even if it was gardening with the others, she'd do her best to help out the Morgan clan as repayment for everything they'd done for her. It was only fair to help their new home thrive.

"Sit," Gunnar ordered, nodding toward the small table. "Let's eat."

Anna Claire sat while Gunnar served up her food. She thanked him and ate the meal he'd prepared. She'd found out he had a love of cooking when she'd first arrived. The meals he made were worthy of a five-star restaurant, but he'd mentioned he never wanted to leave the clan to pursue a career in a big city.

"I'd love to see Ada and Thane as soon as they are out of hibernation," she mentioned as she dipped her chicken in honey Gunnar had put in a bowl for her. He remembered her doing that from the summer, and it warmed her heart.

She'd never had a male care for her. Her own father had forced her to do her own cooking, cleaning, and learning on her own since her mother had passed away. She clamped down on the need to cry for her mother. It'd come to her attention, after she'd been saved by Gunnar and his brothers, that her father had actually killed her mother. She wished she'd been the one to put a bullet between the male's eyes.

It didn't matter. She was safe now, and she had a

new family. Her cousins were there, and she would forever be grateful for that. Ransom and Luca had been treated harshly by their uncle, and she hated how they had been threatened with their lives whenever they came back from searching for Ada with no news. They'd been throwing Robert off her trail, giving Ada the chance to escape Anna Claire's father, who'd sold her to a werebear in Montana.

"Can I get you anything else?" Gunnar asked, breaking Anna Claire from her thoughts. When she glanced at Gunnar, she saw worry and a bit of anger in his eyes. She wanted to console him and let him know not to worry about her. She had to get over the past on her own.

"Can I have more chicken?" she asked, resorting back to her old habits of flinching when she asked for anything. "Sorry."

"Anna Claire," Gunnar sighed, sinking down into his seat. "Look at me, honey."

He'd called her "honey" ever since the day she'd asked for it to dip her meat into. A soft blush painted her cheeks at the memory. "I'm really sorry, Gunnar. Old habits are hard to break."

"I don't ever want you to ask me for anything," he stated. "You have your own free will, and if you are hungry, I will provide food for you until you are no longer starved."

He didn't wait on a reply, taking her plate to the kitchenette and plating another piece of chicken. The male scooped up the jar of honey on his way, placing it next to her bowl on the table.

"Thank you," she replied and resumed eating.

After they were done, Gunnar wanted to step outside to check their immediate land. The Morgans lived on about a hundred acres, and they owned three thousand more for their crops. They'd bought the neighboring property last summer when the elders and O'Kellys joined the clan. That gave them enough room to roam in their shifted forms.

"I'll go with you if you'll give me a moment to put on my shoes."

"Go on," he said. "I'll clean up our dishes while you're getting ready."

The idea of going outside excited her. It'd been a long winter of sleep. She hadn't left the quarters but one time since mid-December, and that was only to see Ada and her new cub, Thane.

She met Gunnar at the front door of the main house as he removed the bar that barricaded them inside. It was a safety measure, and she was glad it was there. It kept curious humans from trying to enter the home because it looked abandoned during the winter months.

"It's warm," she announced as he pulled the door open wide. Off in the distance, Anna Claire saw the darkening sky. "Storms are coming, too."

"We won't be out here long," Gunnar promised. "I just want to check the equipment and our vehicles."

She followed him off the porch and tried not to step on any muddy areas in the yard. It must've rained already that morning, because there was standing water making puddles scattered across the front part of the Morgans' land. Well, she guessed it was her land now, too.

As they rounded the house, Gunnar glanced back at her as she hopped over a puddle. "You need some rubber boots."

"I do," she replied.

They checked the locks on the barn, and Anna Claire leaned against the side of the building while Gunnar went over a few of their plows. She didn't know much about the equipment other than what she'd overheard them talking about at the end of the season last fall.

"Let's check the cabins while we are out." Gunnar paused when the thunder rumbled louder. That storm was coming, and it was coming quick. "Come on. We need to hurry or we will get caught in the rain."

They hurried to the road leading to the new cabins. There wasn't a sound coming from any of them, and they figured the elders and O'Kelly brothers were still in their hibernation. "We can check on them next…"

A loud boom sounded, cutting off what Gunnar was going to say. He grabbed his leg and bent over at the waist. She was about to ask him what was wrong when she looked down and saw blood staining his denim jeans.

"Run, Anna Claire! Get to the house, now!" he snarled, his eyes changing over to the golden hue of his beast.

She gasped and started to reach for him when another boom sounded. The roar from Gunnar was enough to drown out her scream as a pain unlike anything else she'd ever experienced bloomed in her shoulder.

Gunnar's beast ripped from his human skin, shredding his clothes in the process. The huge beast stood over her tiny form as she fell to the ground. The bear didn't touch her, but he did use his body as a shield. Voices sounded from the cabins as another gunshot woke her cousins from their winter sleep.

"Anna Claire!" Ransom yelled as he ran toward them with super speed.

"Someone is shooting at us," she screamed, hoping they'd take cover.

Luca and Ransom ducked low as the next shot sounded, missing all of them. Another round hit Gunnar's bear, but the beast just roared and jerked from the impact.

"Move, Gunnar!" Luca shouted, getting the bear's attention.

When it turned around, Anna Claire cried out from the amount of blood coating the animal's left back leg and side. Luca scooped her up and made a run for the backdoor of the main house just as Rex and Drake's bears leapt from the back porch. They gave him cover to get her inside.

The moment they were safely tucked away, she tried to get out of his hold to look for Gunnar and the others, but she was pulled back by her cousin. "You can't go out there. Let them find whoever is shooting at the house."

"What is going on?" Ada asked as she entered the living room from her quarters. She gasped when she saw the blood coming from Anna Claire's shoulder. "Oh, my gods, you've been shot."

"I'm fine," she promised and took the rag Luca handed her. "It went through. I can shift and repair it, but the males are outside hunting the people who did this. Gunnar's been shot, but I think he's okay."

Gods, please let him be okay.

"He was still standing when we got you out of there," Luca reminded her. "Ransom is helping them look. I'm staying here with you until we get an all clear."

He hurried to the front door, barring it again and closing the blinds. They didn't want anyone to be able to see inside the house. "Now, let me look at that shoulder."

"It's fine, really," she promised, pushing the rag harder against the bleeding wound. Luca came over and inspected the area, sucking air through his teeth when he got a look at the exit wound.

"You need to shift," he reminded her.

"We should go to our quarters," Ada suggested. "I'll tell Tessa to lock herself and Aria inside until they return. Anna Claire, you really should shift and heal that wound."

Ada was right. She needed to shift, and Gunnar's quarters were large enough she wouldn't break anything as she shifted back and forth a few times to mend the wound.

"Luca, come with me to Gunnar's quarters, please?" she pressed as another shot was heard. She bit her lip to keep from screaming out in fear at the possibility the males had been fatality wounded. Gunnar had already taken two healable wounds, but what about the others? Would they be okay?

"You go on down and I'll stay up here," he replied, pushing her toward the corridor leading to Gunnar's room. "Everything is going to be okay, Anna Claire. I promise."

She nodded and ran toward her room, closing and locking the door as soon as she was safely inside. All she could do was pray to their gods to keep the males safe while they searched for the people responsible.

She didn't hear the roar of the bears as they fell to their knees from the bullets pelting their bodies.

Chapter 2

Gunnar's beast took another hit, but it wasn't going to stop him from killing the human males who'd been shooting at them from the wooded area across the road. Drake and Rex, despite their injuries, had taken off to loop around the wooded area of their land, coming out on the road just over a small hill. They'd sneak up behind the shooters and take them out if Gunnar and Ransom couldn't get to them by using the trees in the front yard for cover.

His beast wanted to run at them, but Gunnar calmed him, telling the animal to be patient for the kill. It would happen, and his brothers would make sure Gunnar was the one to take their lives for harming his female.

Anna Claire was too perfect to be harmed, and those assholes had put a bullet in her arm. He shook the image of pain that bloomed on her face the moment she'd been hit. Blood splattered from her shoulder, landing on her thin face. The blood stained her pouty lips, and he wanted revenge for that alone.

Gunnar's beast snarled at the possible pain she was in, but they both knew her wound wasn't fatal. Hopefully, Ada and Tessa were watching her as she shifted to heal. He already knew Luca, her cousin, was there to assist.

The bullets were coming faster, and the beast was losing blood with each hit. There was no way the shooting was coming from game hunters. There were too many shots being fired toward their land for it to be random.

Keeping his head low, Gunnar's bear found shelter behind a stack of firewood where it'd been left between two large oak trees. His gaze landed on Ransom. The young bear had shifted, forcing his healing to begin as he used another tree in the yard for cover. In his human form, he could hide easier.

Loud screams sounded as his brothers attacked the humans, giving Gunnar and Ransom a chance to charge across the street. Ransom shifted and ran with him despite his injuries.

Cool pavement met his bear's paws, but the beast didn't falter as he jumped across the ditch and low fence toward the neighbor's land. They knew the old man who owned the land. It'd been in his family for fifty years, and he didn't want anyone past his fence for any reason. Old man Miles didn't like anyone.

Gunnar's beast lifted his nose when the scent of weapons and blood filled the air. Beyond the small meadow, his brothers' bears were standing over their kills. Three human males lay on the ground with blood oozing from what was left of their throats.

Gunnar's beast huffed at the loss of the kill, but he roared with the victory anyway. Anna Claire had been shot, and he was worried for her. But the need to kill the threat outweighed everything.

"Get the ATV," Drake ordered as he shifted. "Grab a set of clothes from my mate and tell her the threat is gone."

Rex's bear dropped its head and meandered off toward the house. He kept to the tree line and out of sight of the road until he was clear to pass.

"Gunnar, go check on Anna Claire," Drake continued, jerking his chin in the direction of the house. "We will take care of things here."

Taking care of things meant they'd bring the bodies back to the house to dispose of them the old way…with fire. They had ways to keep the scent of burning flesh down so the humans wouldn't be snooping around their lands.

He followed his brother's path and came upon the house as Rex was walking out with a stack of folded clothes and the key to the barn hanging from his finger. "She's okay, but she's asking for you."

Gunnar pushed at his bear, demanding he allow the shift. The beast was exhausted, but knew they needed to shift to heal. He had lost count on how many times he'd been hit before Drake and Rex were able to stop the humans from killing them.

He accepted a pair of shorts Rex removed from the top of the stack and pulled them on as he limped into the house. Shifting was needed, but he wanted to see Anna Claire first.

"Gunnar!" she gasped as he entered the house. Gunnar steadied himself for the impact of her running toward him, but it never came. "Oh, my gods!"

"Shh," he cooed, thankful she held off on the contact. Touching her was a dream, but that moment wasn't the right time. Honestly, he didn't know when a good time would be, either. They hadn't discussed it in months. "I'm fine. Just need to shift."

"You're still bleeding," she observed as she swiped at her beautiful brown eyes. He wanted to reach out and steady her hands, but he leaned over just a little to catch her eye.

"Are you okay?" he asked, ignoring her worry to focus on her. She appeared to have shifted already. He motioned toward her shoulder and waited for her to pull the sleeve up so he could see her wound. A deadly growl bubbled up from his chest when he noticed she hadn't healed enough. "Come, shift with me. You need to heal more."

His order was a little harsh, and it made her flinch, but she nodded and followed him out to the back deck. The beast rumbled inside his head as it prepared for release. The shift was quick, and he turned toward the beautiful female grizzly sitting to his left.

The bear sniffed the air, looking for any threats. Anna Claire's scent was stronger with mating season upon them, and it overpowered the oncoming rainstorm. Thunder rumbled off in the distance, but with each flash of lightning, he knew it was getting closer.

Gunnar fought against his animal's desire to claim her. He knew it was his natural need to find his mate during mating season. A rumble bubbled out of the bear's chest as a sign he wasn't happy at being told to stand down. The human side won out, and the bear rested on his belly while the animal and superhuman abilities worked their magic on healing the gunshot wounds to his body.

He watched over her as she shifted two more times to finally heal the bullet wound to her shoulder. When she returned to her human form, his female dressed and sat across from him as he worked through the changes to heal himself. For once since the first shot rang out, Gunnar was at peace knowing she was unharmed.

Gunnar stood quickly from his seat as the sound of a car pulling into their driveway alerted them to a visitor. He held his hand out for the females to stay put as he checked the shotgun by the door. "It's Gaia?"

He didn't sound upset about this Gaia female, but he did act confused. Anna Claire didn't know who

Gaia was, and she prayed the stranger was on their side. They didn't need any more surprises.

"I've been calling you for the past hour!" The woman stormed through the door as Gunnar held it open wide. She was older, maybe in her forties, with long, black hair. Anna Claire covered a gasp when she took a look at the female's eyes. She wasn't anything like them. No, she was different.

"Yeah, well, we've been busy," Gunnar snarled. "We were just hunted by three humans."

The female launched into a volley of curses and covered her face with her hands. "The sheriff had a vision about that happening. That's why I've been calling you."

"The sheriff?" Drake rumbled as he stood from his seat at the head of the table. "He has no business in our affairs."

"Well, he said the visions are a gift from the gods." She paused to roll her eyes. "He was sent here to watch over those panthers…not you. That's my job."

"You're an angel?" Anna Claire breathed as she stared wide-eyed at the female.

"Ahh, you must be Anna Claire," Gaia cheered, her anger fled and a smiled replaced it.

"Yes, ma'am." She was so confused. What the hell was going on here?

"I am not an angel," Gaia replied and came over to hold out her hand. The Morgan brothers stiffened as she approached. There was something about the female that put Anna Claire at ease, but she couldn't place it.

Scenting the air, she hummed at the smell of wildflowers and rain. The woman's eyes calmed and turned a beautiful emerald green. The swirling was kind of weird.

"Take my hand, child." Gaia gave her hand a little shake in Anna Claire's direction. She wasn't sure if she should, but when the brothers relaxed, she went ahead and placed her fingers into Gaia's. She started to stand, but a vision bloomed in her mind's eye and she dropped back into her seat.

"Oh," she breathed.

The sight before her was nothing like anything she'd ever seen. The earth in all its glory; beautiful fields of flowers, rain forests, and snow-topped mountains. "You're Mother Nature…Mother Earth?"

"Yes, my dear," she smiled and squatted. "I have been a friend of the Morgans' since their mother was a young cub. I made a promise to her that I would always watch over her cubs if something should ever happen to her, and I've kept that promise up until today."

"Don't blame yourself," Gunnar urged, coming to her side. He held his hand out for Gaia to stand, and she took it without question. Anna Claire frowned at the ease with which they made contact. She wished she could do that with Gunnar, but she wasn't ready.

"What happened?" Gaia asked as she looked around the room.

Drake filled her in on what had transpired earlier, leaving nothing out. Hearing the story sent shivers down Anna Claire's spine. The human males were armed to the teeth with ammunition.

"The humans know you exist now," Gaia informed them, quieting as the sounds of the beasts growled and roared into the air. Anna Claire felt the hair stand up on the back of her neck at the news.

"Where are the humans now?" Gaia asked.

"The bodies are being disposed of as we speak." Drake's eyes shot toward the back door, but returned to face the woman who protected them.

"Let me handle that," she offered, but held up her hand when the males made a noise of protest. Her eyes did that swirl thing again, and Anna Claire thought it reminded her of the satellite image of a hurricane. "I have my ways."

Anna Claire was sure she did. Holy hell! She still couldn't believe her eyes. The vision she had projected was beautiful, and she hoped one day she could see all those things with her own eyes. Her beast sat up in her mind at the thought of running free in the mountains of Alaska.

Just as Drake was walking Gaia to the back door, she froze and looked up at the elder Morgan. "Wait, you said three humans, right?"

"Yes, ma'am, why?" Drake responded, his brow furrowing.

"The sheriff specifically said there were four human males," she gasped.

Chapter 3

Once Gaia finished with the bodies, the males returned to the main house. Rex and Drake took their cubs from their mates and sent Tessa and Ada off to their quarters to rest until dinner was ready. Gunnar planned a huge meal for everyone and had made sure the elders and O'Kelly brothers were invited.

"Want me to help?" Anna Claire asked. He wanted to have her in his kitchen helping with a meal, but that wasn't his nature. "Have a seat and relax. You've been through a lot today."

"And you haven't?"

"We've both healed, but I'd feel better if you took it easy," he suggested. He wanted to be gentle with her, and he wanted to spoil her, but he was quickly learning Anna Claire didn't like to sit still for long.

"I'm feeling fine, Gunnar," she whispered. "I wish you'd let me help you prep."

He sat the knife aside and dropped his chin to stare down at the beautiful, blonde female. "You can cut up the carrots."

Sucker!

Gunnar couldn't deny that female anything. He was trying his hardest not to be too overbearing. He was a large male, and with Anna Claire being so tiny, he was worried he'd hurt or frighten her in a way that would set her back.

She washed her hands and took the knife he offered her. She stood in front of the cutting board and pressed her hips into the counter as she began cutting the carrots into pieces for the roasted chicken dish.

Gunnar tried not to watch her, but he found himself mesmerized by the way she handled the knife, cutting the pieces to expert precision. "Where did you learn to cut like that?"

"Online videos," she said with a shrug, then frowned. Gunnar wanted to ask her where her mind had just gone, but she swallowed hard and continued. "After my mother died, I was in charge of the duties at home. I didn't know how to cook, and he allowed me to look up recipes online to learn."

"How old were you?" he asked as he carefully picked up the knife to resume working on the ingredients for his meal. The mention of her father sent a fiery rage through his body, and if he didn't control his anger, he'd use the knife to stab the damn chicken he was planning to cook for dinner.

"Twelve," she replied sadly. He could see the shame and hurt in the way her body folded in on itself.

"Well, you don't ever have to cook again if you don't want to," he offered.

"That's not it," she replied, finally lifting her gaze. There were unshed tears in her eyes, and Gunnar felt his beast push at his skin to comfort her. "I want to care for my mate someday, and even though the reason why I learned to cook is a bad memory, I want to use it for good. Like taking care of…you, Gunnar."

"I am honored you want to care for me," he said after a long pause. "But first, we need to work through a lot of things to get to that point."

"I know," she sighed and dropped her own knife, turning around to lean her perfectly rounded ass against the countertop. "We need to talk about us."

"We do," he agreed with a nod. "But only when you're ready."

"It's mating season, Gunnar," she reminded him, folding her arms across her chest. "We are going to be fighting the call to mate more and more as we get farther into the season."

"I can wait for you," he promised as he moved from his spot by the stove. He stopped only inches from the female, inhaling her unique mating scent. It was a scent only made for him, and it was one he would know anywhere.

"I don't want you to wait," she whispered as she stood tall. "I've come to a realization that what was done to me was done so by some very bad men. It shouldn't define who I am. It's been almost a year, Gunnar. It's time I move on with my life."

Gunnar was four years her senior, but he felt younger than her. She was smarter than anyone even realized. At twenty-two, she should be out partying with her girlfriends and not recovering from the brutality brought on by her father and the men who worked for him.

"If you'd like to talk more, we can do so in our quarters after dinner," he offered. With the humans shooting at them, he would've suggested they take a walk in the woods after their meal, but he didn't want to put her in danger again. They could say what they needed to say to each other in the privacy of their room.

"I'd like that," she replied. Just as she turned away, he saw a dusting of pink across the tops of her cheeks.

They worked together for the next fifteen minutes, and Gunnar found himself smiling more than he had in a very long time. Anna Claire was perfect in every way. He wasn't just saying that because she was his mate. She really was everything he'd ever hoped he could find in a female.

"We have forty-five minutes," he stated, wiping his hands on a towel he kept in his back pocket. "Would you like to retire to our quarters until dinner is ready?"

"I'd like that." She nodded and finished cleaning off her cutting board and knife. He waited until she had put the items away before holding out his hand in a silent gesture for her to go ahead of him.

As they entered the living space, he saw his bed on the left where they'd pushed it against the wall. His couch and chair were closer to the television that hung on the wall by the entry door.

Anna Claire took a seat at his small table just to the left of the door after grabbing a water from the fridge. The female crossed her legs and took a drink, but he noticed she was thinking hard about something. One thing he'd learned about Anna Claire, once she'd healed from the physical injuries she'd sustained last spring, was the female wasn't afraid to speak what was on her mind.

"Gunnar," she began. "I want you to know that I'm ready for you to touch me."

Okay, she had said it. She had told the male she was ready to find out if they were truly mates.

Anna Claire fisted her hands to keep them from shaking at the words that had fallen from her mouth. Gunnar was *huge*...like really, really *huge*. She was only three inches over five feet and he towered over her. The thought of their mating sent a thrill and worry through her bones.

The elder females had said the first mating was

rough…intense. Would she be able to handle him?

"I know you want me to touch you," he sighed, pinching the bridge of his nose after taking a seat beside her. "But, Anna Claire?"

"Yeah?" she replied, unsure of what was going through his mind.

"I need to know what exactly happened to you at your old clan," he ordered, his eyes glowing with the presence of his bear.

She wasn't scared of the bear's presence. In fact, she felt safer…more at ease, knowing the bear was protective of her. For once in her life, she finally had someone on her side she could trust.

"They touched me, but they didn't…well," she paused to grit her teeth, "they didn't take my virginity."

Gunnar dropped to his knees as a loud breath whooshed from his lungs. "Thank the gods."

"I fought them," she continued. Anna Claire didn't want to look weak. She wanted her possible mate to know she was pure for him. "The night I ran away, he touched me all over, but he never did that. I fought as hard as I could, kicking him in his…well, ya know."

She felt tears prick at the backs of her eyes. She hated reliving that night, because she'd never been more scared than she was when he had taken a knife to her body. "He was in too much pain to mate with me."

"I'm…I'm so sorry this happened to you," he choked out.

Gunnar's mating scent swirled around her, and it thickened in the air. She inhaled deep and dropped to her knees in front of him, so they were on an even level. "That time is over. I only told you so you wouldn't think I didn't want to be with you."

"But you've been so sad," he said, looking into her eyes. His bear was close to the surface, and she could see his eyes shifting from human to animal.

Anna Claire wanted to console them both, but she didn't know how…other than to touch him.

"I have been sad," she agreed. "I went through a lot. It wasn't until our hibernation that I really put things into perspective and dealt with what I'd been through. I'm a lot stronger than you all give me credit for. My cousins, they coddle me, and while I love them dearly, I really wish they'd let me get through this my way."

"And what is your way?" he asked. She loved hearing him talk. In the early days, when she'd first arrived, his deep baritone voice kept her steady. It rooted her in place just enough to not go into a downward spiral. She didn't think she'd ever be able to tell him exactly how much he'd helped her.

"I don't let the past define who I am," she stated, holding her head high. "Please, don't mourn for me or what was done to me, Gunnar. I need you to help me celebrate being here…in your clan. I'm happy and safe with you, and that's all I've ever wanted in life."

"I promise to protect you until I no longer walk this earth, and when we reunite in the heavens, I vow to guard you for eternity."

"You really are my mate," she stated.

"I am," he declared, rising to his feet. "Dinner is almost ready. We have all day tomorrow to discuss this some more."

Anna Claire hoped tomorrow would be the day they finally made their mating official. It was well past time for her to move on with her life.

Chapter 4

Gunnar reached for the spoon handle and immediately closed his fist. The beast inside him vibrated with need from Anna Claire's scent. Mating season was here, and he was fighting his nature every moment of the day.

He'd found his mate; had even begun to possibly love her. Despite what she had told him, he still didn't think she was ready for a mating. The males were naturally aggressive when it came to mating for the first time. The females were built differently, and Anna Claire was no exception.

Every single time he thought of her tiny body, the image of finding her restrained in those woods would flash in his mind's eye. That day would forever be etched in his brain. The thought of being aggressive with her during their first mating scared him.

He'd called out for his brothers to cut her down the moment her scent had hit him. Somehow, his bear had immediately known. Seeing the abused female that was meant to be his for life had changed him. No longer was he the rough and tumble youngest Morgan brother. Now, he was softer, more patient than he'd ever been. Call it a growing up phase, but Gunnar saw the difference in himself when he looked in the mirror.

For being in his mid-twenties, he looked older, felt wiser. Anna Claire had calmed him once she had healed from her physical injuries. They'd become close over the summer, and when it'd come time to build her a cabin, they'd both hesitated when Drake had come to ask about her building plan. She'd shyly asked if she could stay with Gunnar during the hibernation, then decide on her future in the spring.

Well, spring had arrived, and they'd finally voiced their knowledge about the mating. It was out in the open now, and it was up to them to decide when to consummate it. She was ready…Gunnar wasn't.

He wanted to make the mating special for her, but how special would any preparation be if he was just going to mount her like a beast after all she'd been through?

Fuck!

Gods, he was so torn.

He plated her chicken and vegetables, taking the dish over to the table. She looked up at him with a smile that tugged at his heart. It was the male's responsibility to care and provide for the females.

Tessa had come to them as a human and refused to let the males provide for her. It'd caused several arguments between her and Drake. In the end, Gunnar had kept his kitchen until the elders joined them. He'd respectfully opened his home to Martha, and during the first few weeks while they set up housing for the new clan members, she'd traded days with him. The moment they'd moved into the temporary housing, and then their permanent home, Gunnar had been back at the stove, preparing the meals for his family.

"This is so good," Anna Claire hummed as she dug into her plate.

When Gunnar turned around, he saw his family gathered around the table. He'd been so deep in thought, he hadn't heard them come in. "It's ready. Y'all come on and eat."

He filled his plate and moved out of the way. His brothers made plates for their mates before making one for themselves. "Has anyone checked on the elders?"

"I called them earlier," Ada announced. "We told them to shelter in place until we know more."

"Are they good on supplies?" Drake asked.

"They are low on a lot of things," Ada frowned. "Alfred said he needed to get to town tomorrow, Friday at the latest."

Drake nodded and set his fork beside his plate. "We need to come up with a plan to find these hunters. There were four in the sheriff's vision, and we took out three. There is one more out there somewhere, and when he comes back, I'm positive he will be bringing friends."

"It's spring, Drake," Tessa huffed, folding her

arms across her chest. "We are low on food and the crops need to be prepared. We have the O'Kelly boys to help, but with this threat, are we going to be prisoners here?"

"No one is a prisoner," he growled, his brother's eyes flashing the golden color of his bear. The air in the room thickened with the male's mating scent, and the females relaxed as Drake walked over to his mate. "We will get the supplies and make sure everyone is cared for. I don't want anyone to worry unnecessarily. There was one missing hunter, and if he returns, we will deal with him."

"Have you thought about calling the sheriff?" Ada asked. "Maybe he has some more insight to his vision."

"You know how I feel about having that lawman on my land," Drake grumbled, narrowing his eyes at his brother's mate. Rex immediately took a stand in front of her.

Gunnar waved his hands in the air to get everyone's attention off his grumpy oldest brother. "We can come up with a plan to get everyone their supplies and not leave the land unguarded."

There was a heartbeat of silence before the males nodded and resumed eating. Gunnar decided to go out and check on the O'Kelly brothers and the elders to take them the dinner he'd promised before the attack. Rex would clean up while he went on his mission.

"Let me go with you," Anna Claire begged after

he'd cleared their plates and made the announcement. She picked up the few containers of food Ada had made for the others.

"It's not safe," he replied, noticing his voice was no softer than Drake's had been when he was upset about the sheriff. "I'd rather you stay here."

"Please, Gunnar," she pleaded, her big eyes staring up at him as if he held her world in his hands. "I need some fresh air, and I'd like to visit with the females."

Gunnar couldn't deny her, and whether she knew it or not, he was defenseless when it came to anything the female wanted. He wouldn't be surprised if his older brothers teased him about being putty in her hands.

"You will have to listen to me about your safety," he grunted. "I want you as close to me as possible."

"I'd be against your skin if we would touch already," she hinted. A soft blush painted the tops of her cheeks as she turned away. "I'll grab my jacket."

Gunnar stared after her as she disappeared down the hallway leading to their quarters. He felt a presence beside him and knew it was his oldest brother.

"You need to claim her before the height of mating season," he warned, giving Gunnar a knowing look when he broke his gaze from the hallway. "She needs you."

"She needs a gentle hand," Gunnar growled. "That isn't me or my bear."

"You underestimate yourself, brother," Rex added. Gunnar finally glanced past their shoulders and saw the females were nowhere to be found. They must've gone to their rooms to give the males a chance to talk alone.

"My bear and I know what we are, and we know our limitations," he replied, running his hand through his long hair in frustration. "But…I just cannot bring myself to touch her yet."

"I don't want to put my nose in your business, but I would suggest you touch her now rather than later," Rex said with a knowing look. "She's more than ready to complete the mating, and you should be, too."

Gunnar glanced down the hallway and took a deep breath, "I'll think about it."

"Don't overthink too long," Drake said in his slow, southern drawl. "That little lady needs you."

Gunnar was quickly realizing he might have been acting too chivalrous. The female had expressed her desire to go through with the mating, but just like a female grizzly, she was waiting for him to make the first move, because that was the way of their world.

"Sheriff?" Gaia frowned when she opened the door to her little home. The damn sheriff knew where she lived, and she didn't like it one bit. "What are you doing here?"

"I came to talk to you," he replied, raising a brow. "May I come in?"

Gaia narrowed her eyes, trying to gauge her trust of the angel. He'd never done anything to harm her or her bears, but his presence irritated her to no end. They were different beings. She wasn't cast down from heaven to care for those in need like he'd been. She didn't even worship the gods. Hell, she was born of the earth, and that had nothing to do with them.

"Sure," she agreed and pushed the door open wide. When he passed the threshold, she felt his power, and it hit her square in the chest, taking her next breath. What was it about that male?

Gaia looked out across her small property and didn't see anything out of the ordinary. The sheriff's car sat in her driveway like a large, white, blinking beacon. She wasn't happy about him showing up in his patrol car. The last thing she needed was for her neighbors to become nosy.

"I came to see you about the hunters," he said, pinching the bridge of his nose. "I don't know why I keep seeing them. They have no bearing on my panthers, and everything to do with the Morgan clan."

"You need to leave my bears out of your

business," she warned as she took a seat in her chair. She pointed toward the couch and waited for him to take a seat. "They are their own people, and they are ruled differently than the other shifters."

"Why is that?" Garrett inquired, shaking his head when she glared at him. "I'm sorry. I'm just curious."

"That's not for us to know," she replied. Honestly, she had no idea why the grizzlies didn't need a leader. There had been speculations over the years, but even she wasn't privy to all of their secrets. "I wasn't sent here by the gods like you were. I'm here on private business."

"Are you ever going to tell me why?" he urged.

"Nope," she replied with a smirk. The sheriff didn't look like he was happy with her short reply. "So, what brings you by?"

"The hunters," he sighed. "There are more of them, and I've found information on the dark web concerning some hackers. They've identified the clans throughout the world, and from my research, it looks like they've killed an entire clan in Alaska."

"What!" she barked as she came to her feet. The news was a shock. "How did they find out about them?"

"I really don't know," he replied with a shake of his head. Gaia began to pace, and the male stood to console her, but she waved him off. "Gaia, it's more than a simple hate group in the local area. They're ganging up and making plans to go after the clans in a mass murder plot of them across the world."

"When?" she demanded, feeling the earth rumble beneath her feet. She knew her eyes were swirling, and it wasn't until Garrett grasped her by the shoulders that she realized there was an earthquake building under her feet.

"Stop," he begged, giving her a little shake. "Gaia, you can't destroy the earth. You're shaking."

"Damn it," she growled, closing her eyes. She slumped into the sheriff's arms as the weight of the news fell upon her. "I can't let them be hurt. I made a promise."

"You made a promise? To whom?" he questioned, wrapping his arms around her shoulders.

"That's none of your business," she barked as she pushed away from the male. The absence of his touch didn't go unnoticed. They both stared at the space between them, and Gaia felt an emptiness she'd never felt before.

"It should be my business, because I keep having visions of your bears," he growled. The sound was so much like the bears, she came up short for a moment. He cleared his throat and backed away. "We have to work together to protect those near and dear to us, Gaia."

"Let me handle the bears," she replied.

"Get them the information, and tell them to stay low," he warned. "Call me if you need me for anything, and I mean it, Gaia."

She nodded and watched as the male headed toward the door. She wrapped her arms around herself, trying to ward off the absence. The male glanced over his shoulder like he was unsure if he wanted to leave but thought better of it and reached for the handle, leaving her with one more order. "Keep yourself safe."

And just like that, the sheriff left her alone in her home, wondering what the hell had just transpired between them.

Anna Claire walked as close as possible to Gunnar as they made their way up the small road the Morgans had cut through their land to the few cabins on their property. The landscape had changed so much since she'd arrived. What was a forest area before, now housed part of her family and old clan. Seeing them every day brought joy to her heart. Having her cousins there helped, but as much support as they'd given her, Gunnar had stood beside her through it all.

"Thank you," she blurted as they rounded the barn that housed their farming equipment. The spring day was a little chilly, and she pulled her jacket tighter around her body.

"For what?" the male asked as the wind blew his long, brown hair around his face. He hadn't shaved in a few days, and that was perfectly fine by Anna Claire. She really wished she could run her fingers across his cheek just to feel the roughness.

"Being patient with me," she replied, looking up into his eyes. He was so tall, but she didn't care. Gunnar was built like a male grizzly should be; tall, thick muscles, and long, flowing hair. She felt an ache between her legs every time he would release his mating scent, too.

"You don't have to thank me," he grumbled, but lifted his nose to the sky. "Your mating scent is strong."

"It's because I want to mate," she said, knowing she shouldn't be so forward, but she was. It was well past time for them to mate. With mating season starting, she was feeling the need to find her mate and make him hers. "Mating season is upon us, Gunnar."

"I know," he replied and looked ahead. "And we will discuss that when we get home."

They were coming up on her cousins' cabin. Ransom and Luca exited as soon as Anna Claire and Gunnar were within hearing distance. They still had a little way to walk before they greeted the males, and she wasn't surprised to see them side by side. Those brothers never went anywhere without each other, and she was glad they were so close. She always wondered how they would be once they were older and found their mates. Would they live together like Gunnar and his brothers? Or would they live apart? Seeing as they were now living in a more welcoming environment, she was sure they'd keep their living arrangements the same once they found their females.

Anna Claire didn't speak about their mating after Gunnar shut her down. They both knew it was going to happen, so why wait? It was driving her crazy. She just knew the male was holding back his true nature when he was around her.

She remembered the day she had arrived and how bad his temper got out of control whenever she was mentioned or seen. It wasn't until she'd properly healed that he'd calmed down. It hadn't been that she saw him often. No, Gunnar Morgan had always been out in the woods, running in his bear form or working in the fields. He'd come in only to cook a meal and eat that first day. After that, he had to start interacting with her because he'd offered her his bed.

The first night she'd tried to sleep in his quarters, she'd tossed and turned from his scent. It was in his sheets and mattress. The damn pillows were worse. It scented of him, and she knew right then and there, Gunnar was her mate. Her bear had claimed him before she ever really knew him.

That was how matings worked in their world. The animal laid a claim, but the first touch was the deciding factor. Once they made skin-to-skin contact, both would know. The magic that made them who they were sealed the mating with an unexplainable connection.

Ransom and Luca were doing okay, but they needed food. As they all walked together to check on the elders, Anna Claire stayed quiet during the males' discussions. The sun was out even though the wind was chilly. She lifted her chin to the sky and absorbed the light. They'd stayed in darkness for almost three months, and she'd missed the warmth.

"We are working out a plan to keep everyone safe," Gunnar promised, shaking Anna Claire from her thoughts. "Drake and Rex are putting together a list of supplies for our home, and we need both of you to do the same. Two of us will go into town while the others stay behind."

"I'll stay with the females," Luca offered. Anna Claire smiled warmly at him. He'd always been protective of the women in the clan. She still hated that their father was so cruel to them and forced them to do his dirty work.

"As will I," Ransom offered.

They checked on both elder couples and waited patiently while they wrote out their lists. Martha sat at her small kitchen table and used a pencil and a piece of paper to carefully construct her list of needs while her mate, Doug, stood behind her. The couple had been together since they were in their early twenties and seeing them at their age gave Anna Claire hope she and Gunnar would find that happiness to last them for the rest of their lives.

"Here you go, dear," Martha said as she handed the list to Anna Claire. The female had been mated for a long time, and she knew better than to hand something off to one of the males.

"We will get your supplies and be back before nightfall," Gunnar promised and shook Doug's hand.

Luca and Ransom promised to be at the house after they helped Doug with loading up some firewood into their cabin. Martha kissed Anna Claire's cheek on the way out. "He's going to be a good male for you, sweetheart."

The whispered words were not missed by Gunnar. He tucked his chin and turned away, pretending not to hear the elderly woman's words. Anna Claire wished she'd known his mother and father. She would've made sure to thank them for raising Gunnar to be respectful to the people who were most important in her life.

They hurried over to the next cabin. Alfred and Peggy Martin were quick with their lists, and Alfred offered to come sit at the house with the females, but Gunnar assured him the O'Kelly brothers were already tasked with protection at the home.

"Just stay inside until we know more," Gunnar suggested. "We will return later with your groceries."

Thanks and handshakes were passed around, and Anna Claire received another kiss on the cheek from the second elder female. Thankfully, she didn't whisper any words of encouragement where the males could hear, but she did give Anna Claire a little wink and finger wave when Gunnar had his back turned.

"Let's head back to the house," Gunnar deadpanned as they exited the elders' cabin. "I don't like us being out in the open this long."

"It's going to be okay, Gunnar," she replied, but accepted the coverage he gave her when he moved to her right side, blocking any attacks from across the road. She didn't know how far guns could shoot, or if the hunters were good enough to sight them in from across the way and down the gravel road leading to the cabins.

"The closer we get to the house, the better chance they have at taking us out," he replied. "I should've made you stay inside."

"But you didn't," she huffed.

"No, I didn't," he confirmed with narrowed eyes. "I can't deny you anything."

"Don't look so upset about that," she teased and kept pace with the male.

"If you get hurt…" Gunnar let the statement hang. She wanted to console him again; take him into her tiny arms and push the hair away from his scruffy face.

Anna Claire wanted to kiss him.

"You'll protect me," she replied, and reached for a hair tie she had around her wrist. Quickly, she bundled her long, blonde hair up into a messy bun and followed him back to the house where Drake and Rex were waiting.

"Rex is staying here," Drake stated as soon as they arrived.

"The brothers will be here shortly, as well," Gunnar announced as he scooped up the list he'd made earlier in the day.

Anna Claire felt a pain in her chest when she realized they were about to leave the land. Gunnar glanced at her and suddenly frowned. "What's wrong?"

"Don't go," she breathed, feeling a panic attack brewing. "You shouldn't leave. What if they're out there waiting for you?"

"They're not," Gunnar promised, coming as close as he could without touching her. "Breathe, honey. It's going to be okay."

Ada and Tessa rushed over to comfort her. She accepted their hushed words, but it didn't change the way she felt about the males leaving the lands. It was dangerous, and they had already had one run-in with the hunters. What happened if they were ambushed on the way to town?

"We have to trust our mates," Tessa whispered as she took Anna Claire over to the table. Ada fixed her a hot cup of coffee and set it in front of her before taking a seat on her other side. The three females held hands as the males made their plans.

She pleaded with her eyes as Gunnar stood across the room. Their eyes were locked even though he held a conversation with his brothers. Soon enough, the males were on their way out the door. She felt tears prick at her eyes, but she held strong. Even with the panic attack wanting to rear its ugly head, Anna Claire had to be strong.

"I think I will retire to my quarters," she whispered, knowing she was going to break down at any moment. The other females hugged her and let her leave just as her cousins were walking in the door. She didn't even stick around to greet them.

Chapter 5

Gunnar sat in the passenger side of his brother's truck as they drove toward town. Next to his leg, a shotgun sat loaded with ammo. They didn't expect any trouble, but with the information they'd been given, the clan needed to be prepared for everything.

"What I don't understand is how they found out about us," Drake grumbled. "We've been careful."

"I don't know," Gunnar sighed. "The sheriff assured us the video of me shifting in that hospital all those years ago was destroyed."

"I believe him," Drake promised, looking both ways at the intersection before making a right on the two-lane highway leading into town. "I wonder if that lawman knows more."

"He could," Gunnar assumed. The sheriff was cunning, and he always had the local panther pride's best interest at heart. He was there to watch over them, and he had no connection to the bears except for the assistance he had given them to get Anna Claire and the others out of her clan. "I wonder if we should pay him a visit."

"If we can find him," Drake answered. "He's probably with those cats."

Drake was interrupted when his phone rang.

Gunnar's hearing was enhanced enough that he heard everything Gaia was telling him. His brother cursed as he reached the town limits, turning toward their old friend's home.

"She said the sheriff stopped by," Drake rumbled.

"Let's find out what he had to say," Gunnar replied, looking out the window. Knowing there was more information relieved him, but it also frightened him. Knowing Anna Claire was out of his grasp agitated his beast. The bear prowled around in his mind, demanding they return to their lands. Gunnar pushed at his bear's mind, forcing it to recess.

"Come in," Gaia said the moment she pulled the door open. Gunnar hadn't been to her secluded little home in a long time. It was during his childhood that his mother would bring him and his brothers to the female's home so she could watch over them when they weren't in school and their parents were working the crops.

"What did Garrett say to you?" Drake asked as they all took a seat in her living room. Her house was small, and she lived in one of the oldest areas of town. Back in their youth, this was the place to be. The area was wooded, and the homes on the tiny roads were tucked away, barely able to be seen from a passing car. Gaia loved her little cottage, and she never expressed a desire to move away. Gunnar assumed since she was nestled amongst the trees with a lake behind her home, Mother Nature was content.

"He came by earlier and told me he'd had another vision," she sighed. "There are hunters all over the world, coming together on the dark web. There is a hacker who has given all of these…haters the locations of grizzly clans all over the world. Somehow, they found out about your kind."

"That's impossible!" Drake exploded, his eyes glowing golden from the presence of his beast. Gunnar reached out and placed his hand on his brother's arm to calm him. He felt the rippling of his beast just under his skin.

"Now is not the time to shift, Drake," Gunnar warned.

"He said there may be more coming, but at this time, he hasn't seen any visions of trouble coming for you until the first of June. There is time to make a solid plan," she offered, calming Drake enough that he took a seat on the couch.

Gunnar's automatic reaction was to glance at all of the open windows in her home to check for anyone who might be watching them. Gaia had them wide open, letting the fresh spring air flow through the house.

"I don't want him in our business unless it's necessary," Drake growled low in his throat.

"Well, I don't think you have an option now," Gaia scolded. "He is the one seeing the visions, not me. You're going to have to set aside your hatred of the sheriff and let him assist you on this, Drake."

"I don't like any of this," he replied.

"We should call him and have him meet us at the house after we grab supplies," Gunnar suggested. "I need to get back on our lands soon, Drake."

Drake knew what Gunnar was feeling. His big brother had felt the same way once he'd mated Tessa. It was the bear's nature to shield and protect, feeling more at home in their territory than anywhere else.

"Call him, Drake," Gaia pleaded, taking his large hands into hers. "I want to protect you, but I don't know how. Garrett's assistance will help me keep the promise I made to your mother." Gunnar's heart tightened at the mention of his mother. Gaia's eyes welled up with tears, but she quickly wiped it away when both males stood.

"We are going to be safe, Gaia," Gunnar promised. The woman had been their protector since their parents had been killed, and she'd always been there for them. "I know it's hard for you to see anything happen to us, but our father taught us well about protecting our lands and mates."

"Speaking of mates," she said past her tears. "How is Anna Claire?"

Gunnar smiled at her because he saw the same twinkling in her eyes that she had when Tessa and Ada had come into their lives.

"She's amazing," he blushed.

"Have you made an honest woman out of her

yet?" she pressed.

"Ah, no," he said shyly.

"Well, you better hurry up," she tsked, looking at her watch. "Spring isn't going to be here for long."

"I know," he chuckled. "Mating season just started. Give me a little time."

"You already love her, Gunnar," Gaia scolded again. She had taken over his mother's duties like a champ even though she didn't have any children of her own. "Claim her."

Gunnar didn't want to get into the reasons for his hesitation. He nodded at the female and stood as a sign he was ready to leave. Drake followed him out after they said their goodbyes.

Gaia was right; he needed to claim her.

But could he bring himself to touch her after all she'd been through?

Anna Claire tossed and turned in the bed. All the females had all taken their leave after Gunnar and Drake had left to get supplies. The males were in the main house, watching over the land. Luca and Ransom were going out to search for foreign scents while Rex stayed back to watch over the house.

She'd felt exhausted after their walk to the

elders' homes, but she never told Gunnar. The hormone spike from the desire to mate was getting stronger, and she knew they'd need to come to an agreement soon. The pain of going through the mating heat wouldn't be pretty.

Anna Claire was already on board, but Gunnar was still worried she wasn't ready. How many times did she have to tell him for the male to understand she knew he was going to be kind and loving to her the first time?

Just thinking about the mating caused heat to pool at her core. Her body felt the need to mate, but he wasn't anywhere around. She didn't have to fight the feelings her body was producing. The heaviness in her breasts and the wetness between her thighs was a clear indicator she was close to going into heat for the second time since she'd come of age.

At twenty-two, she was still scared of what would happen to her during the spring. Last season, she was forced to sit in the kitchen chair at her house while her father stood by, watching while strange men came to their land to touch her. He wanted to breed her for the next generation, and she'd prayed to the gods that none of them had been a match for her.

Thankfully, they had listened, but not before she'd been treated so badly by one of her own clan. The night Dwayne came for her in those woods, Anna Claire's life had changed. She was cut open by his claws and touched by his human hands. If it wasn't for Ada sending her mate, Anna Claire would've most likely died that night.

With each of her limbs tied to two trees and a spiked collar around her throat, she couldn't shift or the spikes would have impaled her. She would've bled out and died within minutes.

A shiver rolled across her skin as she pulled the blankets tighter over her shoulders. The ache between her legs pulsed and she pressed them together. She was definitely going into heat, and without Gunnar there, she was going to suffer until he relieved her. She was tempted to call one of the elders to see if the females could find a sedative, but having them leave their homes would put them at risk. If the hunters were still out there, they could be shot, and she wouldn't put them in danger.

"Oh, Gunnar, why won't you touch me?" she whispered as the heat began to fade. She let out a breath she didn't even know she was holding. The next round of heat would hit more and more the closer she got to her peak. It could be five to ten days before she was over it, and by then, Gunnar would know. There would be no way he wouldn't sense it. Although they hadn't touched, the male would be riddled with lust, and knowing Gunnar like she did, he'd do everything he could not to touch her while she was fertile. He would say the mating would be too much for her to handle.

Closing her eyes, she tried to let the exhaustion

take her away. She needed to sleep for a little while, and maybe, just maybe, the heat would somehow go away.

A rumble woke her from a dream. It was a good dream; one where she'd lived a full life before coming to the Morgan clan. The sound echoed through the room again as she shook the sleep from her fogged brain.

"Gunnar?" she mumbled as she opened her eyes, blinking against the darkness.

"Your scent has changed," he growled. His eyes were glowing, and even in the dark, she could see his body. It'd swollen, his shoulders tight with bulging muscles. His mating scent mixed with hers, and she moaned when the ache between her legs increased.

"I'm going into heat," she moaned. "Either mate me or sedate me, Gunnar. I am in no condition to discuss this with you." She was horny…and exhausted. Her bear wanted the touch of her male to ease the mating fever, and the last thing she wanted to do was to argue with him.

"I can't…" Gunnar cleared his throat, and she closed her eyes, because Anna Claire didn't want to see him walk away. If she did watch him leave her to suffer, she would lose her mind. Crying wasn't going to solve it, and she hated shedding tears, anyway. She'd done enough of that over the last year.

"Just go, Gunnar," she growled, baring her canines at him. They were thick in her mouth, and she felt her bear pushing for release. She fought the change, but it was hard. "Gods, just leave me alone."

"I can't sedate you, Anna Claire," he finally said. She risked a glance in his direction, and when she saw him strip off his shirt, a new, stronger heat surged inside her body. "You are my mate, and I want what's best for you. Tell me if you're not ready. I need to know now."

"I'm ready," she panted as he popped the top button of his jeans.

His long, brown hair hung over his shoulders in waves. Oh, how she longed to run her fingers through it and the short beard he'd kept neatly trimmed over the past few weeks.

"Can you stand?" he asked, frowning when he approached. "I want our first touch to be with us eye to eye, Anna Claire."

"Oh, Gunnar," she sighed and tossed aside the covers. She didn't look very sexy in her yoga pants and tank top. She guessed, at that point, it really didn't matter. If what she knew was to happen, the moment they touched, there wouldn't be anything else to focus on besides making love and marking each other.

She steadied herself, despite the ache between her legs, and stood tall and sure in front of the male. He'd been so hesitant over the last year. The last thing she wanted to do was show any body language that would make him think she was scared or unsure.

"Anna Claire," he breathed as he raised his hands, cupping her face tenderly.

The shock of his touch sent her body to the floor, but he quickly scooped her up and pressed his lips to hers. Magic swirled around them, an invisible bind wrapping around their bodies as their inner bears snarled with something between excitement and primal need.

Her back met the mattress, but she didn't care. There was nothing to be afraid of with this male's touch. The attack she'd been through couldn't be compared to what she was doing now. Gunnar was her mate, and those men were nothing to her anymore. Their brutality didn't hold any weight over her life once Gunnar touched her for the first time.

"Gunnar, please," she mumbled repeatedly until he finally came closer. His eyes searched her own, and once he found what he was looking for, he took her lips again. If that was all she got from him for the rest of their lives, she'd be happy. Kissing Gunnar was going to become one of her favorite things.

His hair was softer than she imagined as he hovered over her, and the short beard he wore rubbed against her skin deliciously. One of his hands released her face and slid down her side, stopping at the waistband of her pants. She didn't want to talk to him for fear it would jolt him out of this mating trance he was in. Lifting her hips, she moaned when he slid his hand around her back to push the material over her ass.

"You are mine," he whispered as if he was thanking the gods.

His touch across her sensitive skin felt like fire, but the burn was welcomed. His lips molded to hers perfectly, and when his tongue snaked out to touch her own, she let out a moan worthy of a seductress.

"Mount me, Gunnar, please," she begged. The ache was building, and her bear was roaring in her mind. They wanted to feel his bite. She'd been told the mating would erase any hesitation once the connection was made, and the elder females had been correct. She didn't care about her past…she didn't worry if he was going to be to animalistic…she just wanted his cock and his seed while he bit into her neck.

"I want to taste more of you," he growled. Gunnar was in his own passion, and when he pushed her tank top off and took one of her nipples between his teeth, she cried out with lust.

Her tiny fingers searched for the fly of his jeans as a growl of frustration fell from her swollen lips. The moment she pushed his jeans past his ass, her hand wrapped around his hardness, and the warmth of it sent her body surging toward him.

"On your hands and knees," he ordered as he pulled away. She didn't have to be told again, because the beast inside her was in charge. The animal knew exactly what needed to be done, and as she got into the position, Anna Claire breathed a sigh of relief. It was finally happening. Gunnar was officially her mate.

His hand ran up her spine, tangling in her long hair. The bear inside her bucked against her skin, but Gunnar was there to hold her in place. It was natural for her to submit to her mate as he broke through her virginity.

She hummed when he rubbed his cock against her wetness, coating himself in her essence. The gasp she'd held in when he pushed against her body came out in a yelp when he broke through.

"Stay still, honey," he cooed. "Let us get used to each other." She knew he was struggling not to move just as much as she was. The pain wasn't as bad as she expected, and the tear to her maidenhood would heal enough not to hurt within a few seconds.

"I can't," she panted. "I need…you. You have to move, Gunnar."

"Yes, my mate," he teased and made one thrust in and backed halfway out before thrusting inside her again.

A storm was brewing inside her body, ready to crash into the earth. The thickness of his cock was just enough to touch every inch of her, giving pleasure without pain. As he continued to thrust, and with each one becoming faster, she fell to her forearms and pressed her face against the sheet. The beast inside her was guiding her, knowing what was going to come next.

He tightened his fist at the back of her head and pulled her up so her back was to his chest. His hot breath sent chills to the skin on her neck as he licked the spot where he would bite her.

"I'm going to mark you," he warned only half a second before his canines sank into her skin.

The storm building inside her rushed out with a gasp. The climax froze her voice, but he knew what to do. Just like every other aspect of her life since coming to the Morgan clan, Gunnar was ready, willing, and able to care for her. As he released her neck, licking over the spot where he'd marked her, her mate fell to his side and pulled her across his body.

"Take me back inside your body and mark me as your own," he whispered, using just one hand to cup her face so she would look directly into his golden eyes.

She took his cock back inside her body and moaned from the feel of it. The slide of his hardness took on a different sensation. With her hands on his stomach, he lifted her hips to teach her the rhythm he desired while she was on top.

"Oh, Gunnar," she said once she finally had a voice again. It was muffled by her canines, but he heard the desire in her voice.

Gunnar turned his head to the side in a silent offering. The beast inside her growled when she saw the spot where his neck and shoulder met. The bear told her to bite him where her mark would be seen by all other females, warning them that he was mated.

She fell to his chest and bit into the spot. A loud roar fell from his lips as she felt his cock begin to pulse inside her. The warmth of his seed calmed her need, squelching the heat.

His blood tasted like his mating scent. The earthy combination of his blood and scent calmed her, relaxed her. When she licked the spot on his neck, Gunnar pulled her back to his lips.

"Hello, mate." He smiled at her, and she found herself returning the gesture with a weight lifted from her heart.

Chapter 6

Sheriff Lynch listened to the radio traffic of a high-speed chase in the northern part of his town. The male was identified as one of the men he'd been looking for regarding the hunters on the dark web group that had been started a few months prior.

Harvey Helms was the only one left in the area from the original four he'd had visions of, but that didn't mean they were in the clear once this male was caught. The information he had found on the group made him sick to his stomach.

They'd killed a clan already and had plans for a mass killing of any and all grizzly clans across the world in the next few months. It was only the end of March, but June first was the date those vigilantes had marked as the "death day" for the grizzlies.

He'd already warned his panthers, but from the information on the site, those hunters were only after the bears. Why? No one knew. From his training, he figured they were honed in on only one species at a time. The fact that the grizzlies had been unknown for all this time upped their chance of becoming famous for bringing them to the media.

Fame and fortune. The greed of it would bring out the worst in humans.

"*Turning south on Pleasant Hill Road*," a voice said over the mic.

The male was running south of town, and that was the last place he wanted Harvey Helms to go. Heading south of town put him in bear and panther territory. While the panthers and bears weren't exactly friends, they had an unspoken agreement to stay off each other's land and out of each other's business. They stuck to that, mostly, unless something big went down and they needed their help.

"Block off Malone Road to the south and run him back this way," Garrett called over the radio.

"*10-4*," his deputy responded.

It was imperative Garrett be the one to arrest the human. He didn't know how he was going to hide this one so the humans didn't get wind of the bears. He had enough evidence to hold him for shooting up the Morgans' land, but if word got out about them, the cool and calm the humans had shown during the original outing of the panthers could blow up in his face.

The bears were deadly, and what made them so deadly was how calm they were. In a split second, your life would be over if you crossed a grizzly. Just like in the wild, they reigned supreme.

"*He's bailing! He's bailing!*" Garrett's curse echoed throughout the patrol car as he flipped on his lights and rushed to the scene.

"Location?" he barked.

When the address was given, he gritted his teeth. He just prayed he could find ole Harvey before those Morgan brothers got ahold of him. Gaia had mentioned they'd shot one of the females, and if Garrett knew them to be like his panthers, the human male wouldn't survive a night out in the woods alone.

In a matter of hours, Gunnar's life had changed. He'd finally given up and touched Anna Claire when he'd come home to her sweet scent. He and his bear had already known what was going on the moment he'd crossed the threshold into his quarters. Her scent had been sweeter…stronger than before.

They'd made a cub their first night together, and he was beside himself with joy. With his nose buried in her belly, his bear rumbled with happiness.

"I can't believe we did it," his mate sniffled. Huge tears welled up in her eyes the moment she'd woken to realize they'd conceived the night before.

"My mate and my cub." Gunnar grinned as he moved from her belly to her lips. "My life is complete, Anna Claire. I've waited for you every spring, and now you're here. I'm going to spoil you both."

"I like being spoiled," she chuckled, but frowned.

"You're not going to let me lift a finger, are you?"

"Probably not," he mumbled, returning to nuzzle against her belly. Gods, the scent of her skin was too addicting. The moment he'd woken up at four in the morning, he had known exactly what he was scenting. His bear had rejoiced alongside him. They'd finally made a family.

"You better not restrict me, Gunnar Morgan," she growled and tangled her fingers in his hair, giving a slight tug so he would look at her face.

"We will have the pride's healer check you out in a few months," he said, knowing damn well he was going to have Harold come over before then to check on his cub. "If he says you and the cub are okay, then you can do whatever you want."

"I feel fine right now," she said with narrowed eyes. "I have a garden to help plant with the females, and you have crops to grow."

"That we do," he sobered, thinking about leaving the house with the hunters still around. "I don't know how we are going to work it out this year. The hunter is still missing, and with him on the loose, I don't want to leave you, or the other females, unprotected."

"You have my cousins," she reminded him. "They're capable of working the crops."

"That's true," he agreed with a nod, scenting her pregnancy again. He buried his nose against her stomach and inhaled. "Maybe they can take over for me for a few weeks. I haven't gotten enough of your scent yet."

Well, who cared if he was as bad as a cat with a fresh pile of catnip? His new mate was making him a father, and he was going to wallow in the newness of the experience. The males would understand. If they didn't, Gunnar would remind them of how ridiculous they'd been when Tessa and Ada were with young.

"I'm hungry," she chuckled when her stomach growled.

His worry for her surfaced, and his brows pushed forward for a moment as he thought of all the recipes he could make for her and his cub to keep them healthy. "You need protein."

"Mmm," she hummed. "Meat sounds delicious."

"Stay here and rest," he ordered as he reluctantly backed away from the bed. "I'll make you something and bring it in here."

Looking at the clock, he realized it was already ten in the morning. They'd refilled everyone's supplies the day before, and he needed to make a large meal for everyone since they'd be at the main house once news of Anna Claire's pregnancy got out.

"I'll call the elders and your cousins," he offered. "We will have everyone over for dinner tonight to celebrate."

"That sounds wonderful," she cheered. The happiness died on a yawn, and he leaned over to kiss her lips one last time before he headed to the big kitchen in the main part of their home.

"Take a nap."

"Yes, sir." She rolled her eyes, sinking down into the covers. Once she closed her eyes, he clicked off the bedside lamp and made his way out.

As soon as he locked his mate in their quarters, the sound of the sheriff's booming voice echoed into the hallway. He narrowed his eyes and put a little power behind his steps as he hurried to the kitchen.

When he arrived, Drake and Rex were already there. Angry scowls tightened their faces as Gaia stood next to the panther's caretaker. "What the fuck is going on?"

A protectiveness like he'd never felt came over him as he stalked the lawman. He already gathered the reason for the male's visit wasn't a good one.

"We found the fourth hunter, but he fled." Garrett sighed like he didn't want to repeat himself. Too fucking bad. "We chased him to a wooded area about five miles from here where he bailed out on foot. I've asked a few of the Shaw pride to help find him."

"Why didn't you call us first?" Gunnar questioned, making fists at his side.

"They were closer," Sheriff Lynch replied with his own narrowed eyes. There was a flash of white in them, but as quick as Gunnar saw it, it was gone.

"We also have some news about these hunters," Gaia stated as she came around the table to stand in front of Gunnar. Her green eyes changed into the swirling blue of her true nature. When they cleared, she smiled brightly at him, pulling him into a comforting hug. "Oh, Gunnar. I'm so happy for you."

"What are you going on about?" Drake grumbled. "We're talking about these hunters."

"Gunnar first," she beamed. "Then the hunters."

"What?" Rex asked, his voice showing frustration.

"Anna Claire and I touched last night," he announced, his smile widening with the news. "We also made a cub."

The cheers could be heard throughout the home. His brothers, and even the lawman, clapped him on the back with congratulations. "I appreciate that, but I need to know what other information you have."

Gaia and Garrett launched into the information the sheriff had found on the dark web. It led them to Harvey Helms, the remaining hunter, but what was uncovered sent Gunnar's protective instincts into high gear.

There were others out there. More than one hundred hunters had been identified across the world. "They're using this dark web group to plan an attack on all grizzlies?" Gunnar had to make sure he'd heard them right.

"We don't know how they found out about your species, but it's been done. Their goal is to kill you and present your bodies to the world. They want fame, and with that fame, they believe they will get a lot of money." Garrett cursed and ran a hand through his short, brown hair. "They even have a document that shows the going price for breaking news photos from each of the major news outlets."

Harvey Helms emerged from the forest not far from the bears' compound. He'd spent the last two days searching for a way to get to them. The forest behind their home was riddled with foot paths where the shifters obviously hunted. Several trees had scratch marks on them, proving their claws were just as dangerous as the grizzlies in the wild.

He needed to report back to the group and make his plans for the first day of June. The hacker had set the date, saying it was the end of their mating season, and if they'd kidnapped any human females, they could be saved before they could turn them into killing machines.

The thought of one of his daughters being caught in their grasp sent an anger through him. The police were no damn help. They were obviously on the shifters' side. Shifters were abominations of God, and Harvey was going to make sure he took out as many as he could before they came for him.

He knew he couldn't use his car anymore. That

damn sheriff was out for him, but he had a plan. There were other grizzly hunters within an hour's drive of his town. He'd placed an emergency call to one of them earlier, requesting a pick-up at the local bar. He was set to arrive around seven. After that, he'd go hide out for the next two months and study the area. He'd already taken pictures of the entrances to the house, plus the three cabins on their land.

Once the first of June came, they'd eradicate the grizzlies and claim their fame as they paraded their lifeless bodies in front of the media. It was time to stand their ground against the devil's pets and send them back to their maker.

Chapter 7

"It's been 3 weeks since you conceived," the pride's healer began. "I'm just going to take your blood and ask you a few questions today."

Anna Claire nodded when necessary and waited for the panther to put on his gloves. She breathed a sigh of relief. The thought of being accidentally touched by a male that wasn't Gunnar scared her to death.

"Just a little stick," he mumbled as he worked. She'd already met the male a year ago when she had been rescued. He was a gentle soul, and she liked him even if the Morgans were apprehensive about the cat shifter being in their home. "How have you been feeling? Any sickness?"

"Just a little in the evenings," she replied with a cringe. Gunnar's bear rumbled from inside his chest. She hadn't told him of the symptoms she'd been having. "It's not bad, though."

"Try some chicken or toast," he suggested. "I'd prefer you get as much protein as possible, but your body will tell you what it needs. My only request is that you stay hydrated."

"I can do that." Anna Claire glanced at her mate, and he was staring intently at the back of the healer's head. She knew they were on edge with the hunters and having another shifter in the house, but they could at least relax a little. The healer wasn't an enemy.

Hell, the Morgans didn't really like anyone other than their own kind. Tessa had told her about their parents one afternoon last summer while the males were away working in their fields. As she glanced at the three brothers standing at attention around her, she really wished they'd accept the friendship the panthers offered.

"Thank you, healer," she said, sweetly. "Would you like to stay for coffee?" She ignored Gunnar's narrowed eyes and focused on the doc.

"While I appreciate your hospitality," he began, giving her a knowing smile. "I have to get back to my pride for another appointment. Maybe the next time I come over, I'll have some extra time to chat."

"That would be lovely," she replied as he removed the needle.

He labeled the vials and put them in his black bag. The tall, older male stood and shook Gunnar's hand. "Congratulations, papa. I'll call Anna Claire after I get these tests back."

She noticed how the doc showed her mate respect, but he announced he would be calling her, instead of Gunnar, with the results. There was a rumor going around about how the female panthers of the Shaw pride were now working as Guardians, and she wondered if it was true. She didn't want to ask him in front of the males, but she made a mental note to slip in the question the next time he stopped by for a checkup.

"Let's get you some lunch," Gunnar offered as he started for the kitchen. The brothers walked the healer out to his truck and returned to their quarters. "Why didn't you tell me you'd been feeling sick?"

The hurt in his voice brought tears to her eyes. "I didn't want you to worry."

"I'll always worry for you," he replied.

Anna Claire stood from her seat and walked up behind him while he dug through the fridge. The moment she slid her tiny fingers under his shirt and around his body, they both shivered from the electric touch.

They'd become friends before they were mates, and she couldn't have asked for a better second half to her life's story. The first part was slowly fading into nothing but a bad memory. Being with Gunnar and his brothers had changed her, molding her into a stronger version of herself.

"What's wrong?" Gunnar stiffened in her arms, and she let out a soft sigh when he turned around to pull her close to his chest. He didn't give her a chance to respond before capturing her lips in a scorching kiss.

"Nothing's wrong," she promised. "Just thinking about how happy I am."

"Good," he stated with a short nod. "Now, let me make you some lunch before I have to relieve Luca from the fields."

Her cousin and Gunnar had taken shifts at the fields during the current planting season. The weather was holding out, and they'd been working from dusk to dawn to get the seeds in the ground.

"Tessa's friend, Tulley, is supposed to be delivering the things we need for the home garden today." Anna Claire couldn't wait to get to work on their plot behind the house. The males had expressed their concern for the females working out in the open, but Tessa had calmed them when she pointed out how safe the location was. They were covered from all sides; the front of the land being the most important. With them directly behind the house, no one could shoot at them from across the road.

The males had gone out to check the land behind the home a week ago, and they hadn't found any lingering scents that would've alerted them to a stranger on their land. They'd had a lot of rain, and any footprints would've been seen, too. There was some concern over whether someone had been on their land before the weather changed since their scent would've washed away with the recent storms. Thankfully, they were safe…for now, but the males were on high alert. The Morgan brothers were always paranoid, and she was starting to understand why.

With the sheriff's knowledge of an attack on the

first day of June, the clan was preparing for the worst. Drake had ordered extra ammunition for their weapons, and a plan was in place to protect the females and young. Doug and Alfred were setting traps around the land, going a bit old school in their hunting techniques.

"Don't linger in the garden," he warned as he set a bowl of homemade chicken noodle soup in front of her. She ignored him and took a bite. The flavor was exceptional. "Luca and Drake will be out there with you."

"I'm not worried," she admitted. "We are relatively safe out there."

They were interrupted by his phone. Her mate frowned as he answered it. "Gaia?"

"Get to the diner now," she yelled in a panic. "It's been shot up." With Anna Claire's excellent hearing, she understood everything the female was saying. There were tears in her voice, and Anna Claire's heart dropped into her stomach.

"Call the sheriff and get to your office," Gunnar barked as he jumped from his chair. His eyes landed on her, but Anna Claire made a fast motion with her hands to send him out the door.

"I'll call the others," she promised and reached into her dress pocket for her phone. Her first call was to her cousin, Ransom. He was at his cabin and could be at the house in the blink of an eye.

Her next call was to Drake. She didn't have

much to tell him other than what she'd overheard from the phone call. When they disconnected, Anna Claire glanced over at her mate, who was pacing in front of the kitchen island.

"I have to go," Gunnar fretted. "Don't go outside for anyone. Do you understand me?"

"I won't. Now, go!" Anna Claire sat heavily in her chair and placed her hand over her erratic heart. He kissed the top of her head and produced keys from his pocket as her cousin came in the back door.

"I don't have time to explain," Gunnar said in a rush. "Stay with the females. I'll call as soon as I know something."

With his phone to his ear, her mate ran out the door. Ransom came over and pulled her into a comforting hug. It was nice to know she could still touch her blood relatives. "Someone shot up Gaia's diner."

"Son of a bitch!" Ransom snarled, running his hands through his long, dark hair. "Do you think it's related?"

"I wouldn't doubt it," she replied.

Gaia cursed as she held a rag to the wound on her arm. Unlike the shifters, she couldn't heal as fast. The only saving grace was that the bullet had grazed her instead of killing her.

The call to the sheriff was met with the same anger as it'd been when she called Gunnar. He'd used his supernatural magic to transport himself to the diner in an instant.

"Talk to me, Gaia," he said in a panic. "Where else are you hit?"

"I'm fine, Garrett," she promised. "It's just my arm."

"Fuck!" the angel cursed, causing Gaia to raise a brow. She wanted to scold him, but she thought better of it when he queued the mic at his shoulder to call for backup.

"Can you get to your office?" he asked her as he glanced around at the patrons who were staring at him in wide-eyed shock before lowering his voice. "I have to take care of the humans."

She nodded and hurried to her office, falling into the chair behind her desk. She pulled the rag away and flinched at the sight. She'd need stitches. If the bullet had been six inches to the left, it would've killed her, and that would've been bad...like bad, bad.

She was the human embodiment of Mother Nature, but she didn't have the extra abilities like the shifters. If she was mortally wounded, it *would* kill her. If she died, so did the earth and all its inhabitants.

The sound of emergency personnel arriving

eased a little of the tension she was feeling. Thankfully, the diner had been slow, and only a handful of customers had been there between the breakfast and lunch rush. From what she'd seen before Garrett arrived, no one was injured. She'd taken the worst of it.

The blood slowed from the pressure she was keeping on the wound, but it wasn't stopping. The moment she went to stand from her seat, she felt a wave of dizziness come over her, sending her ass right back into the seat.

"Woah," the sheriff gasped as he entered her office. "You're white as a ghost."

"Blood loss," she frowned. "I need another towel. There are some under the sink."

"What?" he asked, going to her attached bathroom to grab what she needed. The male looked worried for once, and that scared her. What had happened outside after she was sent to the office? "Why aren't you healing?"

"I won't heal like them," she admitted, accepting the towel. The sheriff produced a pair of blue latex gloves from his pocket and quickly put them on. "Let me look at it."

When she pulled away the new towel, Garrett narrowed his eyes. "Why don't you have their healing abilities?"

"I am Mother Earth," she reminded him, refraining from rolling her eyes. "I heal as the earth heals…with time."

"Are you serious?" he snarled, his eyes flashing white. The angel inside him was rearing its head, and while she appreciated it, she didn't really want to discuss too much of her life with the lawman.

"Look, Garrett," she began after a long sigh. "I need stitches. There is no need for an antibiotic. I can use the earth for any infections I might get from the wound."

"Can you go to a human hospital?" he asked as he swatted her hand away from the rag, using his gloved hands to put pressure to the wound.

"I…I really don't know," she answered. Honestly, she didn't know if they would question her should they draw blood. She was in human form, but she didn't know if her chemical makeup was the same as the humans. "I don't want to risk it, though."

"Well, someone out there knows about you," he growled. "This had to be connected to the bears. No one shoots up the town. We don't have that type of violence here."

Garrett was right. Olive Branch was a safe, quiet little town. They'd had some run-ins with a few bad eggs, but they were mostly from the Memphis area, trying to come across the state line to look for more homes to rob, but the sheriff's department had kept that to a minimum.

"Whoever it is, I want them found, Garrett," she ordered, feeling her eyes swirl. "They came here to hurt me, and in the process, they hurt humans."

"The humans are fine," Garrett assured her, taking a peek at the wound as he knelt at her side. "No one was injured."

"Still, they were attacked, and I don't want them to be scared to come here," she fretted. Gaia loved the humans. Well, the good ones. The ones who destroyed her earth were the lowest of scum. Whoever shot up her business was going to be grouped into that category as far as she was concerned.

"Let me call the pride's healer to come here and stitch you up," Garrett offered. "I don't think you should be going to the hospital."

"I think you're right," she replied, and hissed when he removed the rag.

"Your bleeding is under control, and that's a good sign," he replied, but his brow was furrowed. The lawman used his other hand to retrieve his phone from his pocket. "You scared me, Gaia."

"I scared myself, Garrett," she replied as he connected the call with the panther's doctor.

"Stay here," the sheriff ordered. "I'll go check on things out front and get someone over here to either board up your windows or replace them before the day is through."

"Thank you."

The door to her office was pushed open as Drake, Rex, and Gunnar entered, stopping in their tracks when they saw the sheriff still holding the rag to her arm. They all started yelling questions at the same time, and she couldn't understand anyone while they growled through their questions.

"Calm down," she warned, raising her free hand in the air. "I'll explain everything."

"Keep pressure on that, and I'll be back," Garrett stated as he nodded toward the bears. She took over with the rag and watched as the male left the office. He didn't even flinch when all three of the Morgan brothers growled in his direction.

"So, what the hell just happened?" Drake bellowed.

"Have a seat, calm down, and I'll fill you in," she promised and relaxed in her chair for the first time since the bullets had started flying in her diner.

Chapter 8

Anna Claire paced as she waited to hear from her mate. Ransom was across the room, rolling his eyes at her. Tessa had been sorting through the package Tulley had delivered half an hour ago, and Ada was watching the two cubs play on the living room floor.

"No news is good news," Tessa reminded her. "If anything happened to Gaia, Drake would've called already."

"I guess you're right," she replied and pressed a hand to her stomach. The thought of someone shooting up her diner made Anna Claire sick. "Do you think it's the hunters?"

"At this point, I'm sure it was." Tessa sighed and dropped the packets of seeds on the table. "The sheriff is working to find out who the hacker is, and I'm positive he's also trying to get the information taken off the internet."

Anna Claire bit her finger as she thought. The dark web was accessible, but what would they search for to find the information the hacker was releasing to the public? She really wished she had more knowledge on computers. Her father had outlawed them, and since she was homeschooled, he limited her time to only looking up recipes from approved sites.

Since moving to the Morgan clan, Tessa and Ada had shown her how to access stores on the internet to purchase clothes and supplies. Gunnar had set her up with a cell phone and taught her how to use the browser to do the same thing. As far as the dark web was concerned, she was as clueless as the day she'd first sat down behind a screen.

"Can any of you find this dark web?" she blurted.

"I have no idea," Ada said with a shrug. Anna Claire knew her friend had been as sheltered as she was when it came to technology. Ransom was no different. The only person in the house that might have any knowledge was Tessa.

"I *might* know a thing or two about it," she hedged. "Drake would kill me, though, if I accessed it from the house."

"Well, damn," Anna Claire whispered. "We need to find out what's going on."

"Don't you ladies be getting into any trouble," Ransom interrupted. "If you dare even breathe toward the dark web, the authorities will know it and they could possibly show up here."

"He's right," Ada scowled. "The brothers would go feral if that happened."

Anna Claire walked over and picked up the seeds, sorting them for Tessa while she stepped away to make some food for Aria, her cub. She glanced over at the female, then over toward Ada, who was nursing her cub, Thane. Her sisters-in-law had a sparkle in their eyes, and she had a feeling Tessa knew a way to access the information without the males getting involved.

"Let's get these seeds planted after the cubs are down for their naps," Tessa announced, jutting her chin out at the back of Ransom's head. "Maybe Ransom can help us pour out all the bags of soil."

"I'd be honored to help," he chimed in, but never took his eyes off the television. He was watching a show about old muscle cars and basically ignoring them.

"I have a way," Tessa whispered as she passed to take her daughter to their quarters. "I'll be right back."

Tessa and Ada spent time putting their cubs down for a nap. Ransom was so engrossed in the show he was watching, Anna Claire was able to finish sorting out the seeds. Once she placed them in stacks to represent each row of their garden, Tessa returned with her hand deep in her pocket.

"Ransom," she called out. "Could you be a dear and get the bags of soil cut open for us?" Anna Claire held back a chuckle at the sweetness of Tessa's voice. She knew the males would do anything for the females of the clan, and they were betting on Ransom leaving the house for a good ten minutes.

"Sure," he groaned and stood from his spot.

Tessa and Anna Claire made themselves look busy and not at all guilty of what they were about to do. The moment he walked out the back door, Tessa pulled a cell phone from her pocket. "Drake is paranoid. So, he has this burner phone and I can access the internet on it."

"Go, go!" Anna Claire peeked over Tessa's shoulder as the female got down to work. Ransom was hauling four of the twelve bags they'd ordered from Tulley. "We don't have much time."

Tessa frantically typed away on the phone's browser. She chewed on her lip for a few minutes and laughed when she dropped the phone on the table like it'd burned her. "Found it!"

"How did you…oh, never mind," Anna Claire said as she peeked at the screen.

The website she'd found looked relatively harmless, but upon further inspection, Anna Claire noticed the words "bear shifter" and "abomination" across several headlines. "What are these?"

"Message boards," Tessa replied as Ada joined them. All three women were crowded together as they stared at the phone. "People post a message and other users can comment under the post."

"Click on that one." Ada's voice held a bit of awe as Tessa tapped the screen. "I want to know what they're saying about us."

A bubble of laughter fell from Anna Claire's lips as they read through the comments regarding the grizzly shifters. "They think we are witches."

"That's funny," Ada giggled.

"What's so funny?" Gunnar asked from somewhere behind them.

The three women yelped and spun. Tessa grabbed the phone and tucked it in her back pocket. Gunnar's eyes narrowed on the three of them, and Anna Claire felt fear race through her veins.

"Oh, hi," Ada said, trying to get Gunnar to look away from Tessa.

"What were you three up to?" he asked, suspicious.

"Nothing," they replied in unison.

"The fact that all three of you look guilty as hell, and I can scent a lie a mile away, proves to me that you females are up to something," he said, holding out his hand. "Hand over whatever you just put in your pocket, Tessa."

"Ah," she hedged.

"Now," he snarled in warning. "Your safety is our first priority, and if you are hiding something that might put you in danger, I, and my brothers, will want to be privy to the information."

"Wow," Ada breathed. "I feel scolded."

"You'll be spanked if you don't hand it over," Drake growled as he walked into the kitchen. Tessa cursed under her breath, but a bright red blush painted the tops of her cheeks. Anna Claire looked away because she didn't want to even know what that was all about.

"Ada," Rex's voice rumbled as he followed the

oldest Morgan brother.

"We wanted to look for the hunters on the dark web," Tessa blurted as she produced the burner cell phone, handing it over to her mate. "I'm sorry, Drake. We wanted to research them and help out in some way."

Oh, Tessa was good.

Drake took the phone and looked at the screen. He glanced at his mate through his long, corkscrew hair. There was a bit of disappointment in his golden gaze. He nodded and slid the phone into his pocket. "This is dangerous."

"I know," she replied.

"The feds could come for you for even accessing the dark web, Tessa," he reminded her.

"That's why she used the burner phone," Anna Claire blurted, wanting to stand beside her friend and sister-in-law. All three of the females were at fault, and she wasn't going to let Tessa take the fall for it. "We really were just looking for clues and gathering information."

"I'm not saying what you did was wrong, because the sheriff is supposed to be looking into this group of hunters. Apparently, the government is working to shut the site down and find the hacker who leaked the information about our species." Drake was frustrated, and Anna Claire felt a little bad for going behind his back, but the females wanted information, too.

"We need to be kept in the loop on these things," Anna Claire began, nibbling on her thumb. "We have cubs, and I'm with young. If these hunters are coming, we need to be ready, and having the information up front will keep us safer than being physically protected by you."

She saw Ada smirk from the corner of her eye. Tessa gave her a wink over Drake's shoulder. All the men stood there in shock at her independent thinking. It was true, though. They needed to be prepared and being informed was a key part of that.

"Maybe I should set up a meeting with the sheriff," Drake mumbled.

"That would be wise," Ada replied, coming to stand next to Anna Claire. Tessa joined them and the males finally relaxed after Drake made the call to Garrett Lynch.

Now, they would wait for the lawman to come around and tell them what they needed to know. After that, Anna Claire would make her plans to keep everyone she loved safe. As she rubbed her flat stomach, she prayed she wasn't bringing a child into a world where they were going to be hunted and treated like the predators the humans thought them to be. If the world started coming for the shifter population, they would succeed. There wasn't enough of them to take on an entire army of humans with guns.

They'd be eradicated.

Gunnar brushed out his long, brown hair, leaving it to dry naturally. He was still trying to calm his beast from catching the females going behind their backs to search the dark web for any information they could find. Drake had confiscated the phone and told the females to let the males handle the information. It wasn't safe to search the dark web, knowing the feds were always watching the internet and the shady things within.

It was late, nearing midnight, when Drake texted him and Rex, planning a meeting in the barn. He wanted to wait until the females were asleep before they conducted their own search of the message boards the hunters were using.

As he entered his bedroom, Anna Claire was fast asleep. She was on her side with her hands tucked under her chin. He traced the soft lines of her face. Her lips were slightly open as she breathed softly in her slumber.

He'd fallen for her the moment he'd laid eyes on her in that forest. The scent of a mate was hard to deny, but he'd done it. He'd become her friend and confidant in her time of need. There wasn't anything they couldn't talk about, and he felt honored the female trusted him after all she'd been through.

The door didn't make a sound as he left his quarters. His hallway was dark, but his vision was perfect once his shifted his eyes to see his way into the main house where he found his brothers waiting in the front living room.

Drake jerked his head to the side, indicating they should follow him. Even with their mates and cubs asleep, the males didn't want to be overheard. There needed to be a plan in place to stop the hunters before they ever arrived on the Morgan clan lands. If they knew about them, then those human males surely knew they owned the largest corn farm in the area. That could cut into their living just as much as if they come back to take them out with bullets.

Drake unlocked the side door to the barn and pushed it open wide, flipping on the overhead light in the process. The hum of the bulbs echoed in the metal building as Rex pulled out three stools from his workbench.

"Have you looked at it yet?" Gunnar asked, nodding toward the phone in Drake's hand.

"Yeah," he sighed. "There is a lot of information on here, but I found something that is going to shake up the community once it's known."

"What's that?" Rex inquired. His middle brother held out his hand once Drake unlocked the screen. A rumble vibrated his chest as he looked up with golden eyes. "They killed two clans."

"One as recently as last night," Drake confirmed.

Gunnar's heart thundered in his chest as he held out his hand. "Let me see."

The information was right there in black and white. They'd posted photos of the dead; two in human form and six others as their bears. Bile rose in his throat as he noticed two of them were cubs. He felt anger and tears pricked at his eyes.

"How could they!" he bellowed, backing out of the screen. "They killed cubs, Drake! What does that mean for us?"

"It means we are going to go find them before they can harm our family," Rex vowed.

They all quieted as they searched for any information leading them to believe there were more hunters coming their way. The clans in Alaska were the biggest target, but the hardest to find because of how remote their homes were in relation to roads.

Gunnar snarled as he saw the information crossed out for Anna Claire's old clan, saying the homes had burned and there had been no sign of activity in the area for almost a year. "They've known about us for a while."

"Looks that way," Rex huffed and pointed to the screen. "Keep scrolling."

Drake searched through dozens of posts, stopping to read most of them. A growl bubbled out of his throat when he found one containing information about the Morgan clan.

Grizzlies south of Memphis, TN – Research

indicates there are three brothers living in Olive Branch, MS. Their land is a short thirty-minute drive from the Memphis airport. Take the highway south of town after you cross over the state line. Drive fourteen miles and turn left at the abandoned corner store. Their land is one mile down on the right. As of this post, the clan consists of three brothers and their two female "mates".

Unconfirmed info: Seven new "members" arrived last spring. No more information as of this post.

"What the fuck?" Rex snarled. "That was dated a week after Anna Claire and the others moved in."

"Keep reading," Gunnar ordered, trying to focus on what information they had about his extended family. If they mentioned Anna Claire by name, he was going to go feral.

Harvey Helms: Those abominations killed three of my men. I have searched their lands while they were away and found three cabins on the land, as well as the main home. I do not have a head count at this time, but I will be watching them over the next few weeks.

"That son of a bitch was on our land a month ago!" Gunnar's bear pushed at his skin to shift, but he held the animal back. "We searched for scents, but we missed him. The rain must've washed it away."

"Hang on, there's more," Rex interrupted, pointing to the phone where Drake had laid it on the workbench.

Skipper Jones: We are not far from you, and we are willing to come help. I have two men besides myself. I will be in contact over a private message.

Harvey replied with a generic thank you and that was all that had been said in the last few weeks. Gunnar automatically shifted his hearing, calling on the bear's extra abilities so he could listen for sounds, but there was nothing. His paranoia was going to cause him to lose his mind again when it came to his mate.

"We have to set up a plan tonight," Gunnar ordered. "Right now, Drake. Someone needs to wake up the O'Kelly boys so we can start our guard immediately."

"I agree," Drake replied, pulling out his personal phone. He called Ransom and waited for the male to answer. Drake filled him in on the information, telling them to come to the barn but to stay silent as to not wake the elders or the females.

The door opened after a few minutes, revealing Ransom and Luca. They walked over to where the phone was laying on the bench and Ransom picked it up to scroll through the information. He cursed several times, and when he looked up, his gaze locked on Gunnar. "They didn't mention Anna Claire, but they know how many of us are here."

"It doesn't matter if they have an actual head

count," Drake reminded everyone. "They know our address…even gave directions to our front fucking door. This is serious, and if those fucking humans want a war, that's exactly what we will give them."

"What do you propose?" Luca asked, his eyes glowing gold just like all the males' in the barn.

"We draw on our nature and eliminate the threat," Drake answered, his voice deeper and darker than ever.

All of the males turned their heads at the sound of tires on their gravel driveway. Everyone growled low in their throats as Drake hurried toward the door. Gunnar's brother relaxed when he noticed who had arrived.

"It's the sheriff," he announced.

The angel killed the lights and engine before he got to the house, rolling to a stop beside Drake's truck. They waited for him to approach the barn before they spoke. No one wanted to make any unnecessary noise to wake the females or their cubs. Gunnar was worried for Anna Claire, but knew she was as safe as could be tucked away in their quarters.

"I need to know what you're planning," he replied. "My visions haven't changed, and based on the one I had earlier, it doesn't look good."

"How bad?" Rex growled.

"If something doesn't change, it will be the total destruction of your species."

Chapter 9

For the past two weeks, the Morgan clan had been on high alert. Anna Claire, Ada, and Tessa were being guarded throughout the day and night while the males kept close watch on their land.

The crops were planted, leaving plenty of time for the males to search for the men who were coming for them in less than ten days. Anna Claire watched as Rex added hooks to the back of the new metal door to her and Gunnar's quarters. A thick metal rod would be fit in place should the human hunters gain access to the house.

Anna Claire had been a bit angry with her mate after she'd found out what they'd done the night the females had been found with the burner phone. They'd taken it upon themselves to get the information and come up with a plan.

She understood their worry, and with her being pregnant, the males were fearful of the worst. Tessa had raised hell until Drake showed her the message boards he'd found pertaining to their clan. Once the females read over the messages, they started making their own plans to keep their cubs safe. It was Ada's idea about the doors to their quarters. If the hunters did gain access to the main house, they'd have to get through the metal doors with several deadbolts and steel bars to keep them closed.

Her cousins were busy working on making accessible basement spaces underneath all three cottages. The finishing touches were being put on Ransom and Luca's home before stocking it with two weeks' worth of supplies.

Anna Claire wasn't able to leave the house for more than a few minutes to check on the garden right behind the house. Thankfully, it was within feet of the back door, but Gunnar was always there with a shotgun at the ready should someone attempt to get to her. She felt safer than she ever had, and even though the hacker had given a kill date of June first, she knew they were going to be okay.

"Let me water them, and we can go back inside," she said to Gunnar, who was watching every open area around the little secluded spot they'd turned into the garden.

"We've been out here long enough as it is," he growled, his eyes glowing with the presence of his bear. The male's canines were thick in his mouth, and while she loved it when he partially shifted, seeing him on edge broke her heart.

She watered the garden and gathered the basket of vegetables she'd been able to pick that day and stood with a groan.

"You okay?" he asked. Gunnar worried over her, but she was perfectly fine. The panther's healer had been by two days ago to give her a checkup. Her bloodwork came back normal, and they were able to hear the cub's heartbeat on the little monitor Harold had brought to the house. In a few months, they would get to make the decision to know the sex of the cub. They were still unsure if they wanted to know. The bears usually lived by the old ways; the males delivered their own cubs during the winter, and they waited until that time to know the sex.

"I'm fine," she promised and waited for Gunnar to open the door. He followed her into the kitchen after leaving the shotgun on a rack above the backdoor. With Aria walking now, they had to keep the guns out of her tiny reach.

"Want some lunch?" he offered as his body relaxed and his eyes returned to their normal brown color.

"I do," she nodded and washed her hands. "Maybe after lunch, we can have some alone time in our quarters?"

"I'd like that very much," he replied as his eyes darkened.

With everything happening, and the increased security, Gunnar had spent a lot of time in the woods behind their home, searching for the human males. The plan was for them to shift and take turns scenting for them and hiding in the darkened areas of the land in the hope that Harvey and his buddies would attempt to return for information.

So far, there had been no sign of them.

"Gaia will be over sometime this evening," she reminded him.

"So will the sheriff," he added, serving her a bowl of his delicious beef stew.

They ate in silence as they shared a meal. Gunnar sat to her right and kept his free hand on top of her knee. The connection was welcomed, and even though she knew his reasoning, she felt more at ease when they touched.

Rex and Ada entered not long after and grabbed themselves a bowl before joining them. They were quiet, and the tension in the air was thick. Everyone was on edge, unsure of what the next several days would bring.

"We are going to retire to our room for the afternoon," Gunnar announced as he took her empty bowl. Anna Claire covered a yawn with the back of her hand and stood from her seat.

Ada and Rex gave them a nod and resumed eating as they walked away. Gunnar took her hand and the mating connection swirled around them. The magic caused a shiver to roll up her arm, and his mating scent sent a wetness between her legs.

By the time they reached their quarters, Gunnar had picked her up and carried her over the threshold with his tongue deep in her mouth and his strong hands gripping her ass.

"We have seven days until the first, but I want to go at them sooner," Harvey stated, sitting on his old, worn couch. It'd been two days since Skipper Jones had arrived with his son, Don. They'd brought their own weapons and were as anxious as Harvey to get rid of the bear shifters.

"I'm ready when you are," Don said with excitement. The kid was barely into his mid-twenties and so eager, it sent a thrill through Harvey. It was about time the younger generation fought for something other than free healthcare and higher pay. Those abominations would rule the world if they spread their species with the humans. All it would take was for them to start knocking up females and the world would be full of them. It was time to take a stand now before things got out of hand.

"I want to know, why didn't they come out with the panthers?" Skipper asked as he rubbed his chin. "There's something fishy about that."

"Whatever the reason is, we won't have to worry about it for long," Harvey stated. "As of the first of June, they'll all be dead."

The two other males made noises that sounded like agreement and headed for their room. Harvey had sent his daughter to her mother's house for the next two weeks, saying he was going to be out of town. He didn't want her anywhere near those bears.

"Get some sleep and we will head out around three in the morning to get more information on those bears," Harvey ordered. "I know how to access their land from the back."

Anna Claire gritted her teeth as Gunnar used his tongue between her legs. The sensations of his hot tongue on her core and his soft hair on the inside of her legs was too much. "Gunnar…oh, Gunnar."

He moaned as he made another pass with his tongue, making her legs vibrate from the love making he was doing down there. Holy shit did it feel amazing. Anna Claire didn't know sex with her mate would be this…intense.

"I can't…" Anna Claire's voice was gone. She couldn't speak coherent words when he was coaxing a release from her body. Her mate had been insatiable ever since that first night, and if she was being completely honest, so was she. "I need you inside me, Gunnar."

"But I like this," he mumbled as he released her. "I like it when you squirm."

A blush painted her cheeks as his golden eyes

caught hers as he watched her over the top of her mound. "I like you…inside me."

She'd been very vocal since their first time. He liked it when she stated what she wanted, and he told her that every chance he got. The whispered words while they worked together in the kitchen were the best. Gunnar liked to get her worked up while her hands were full of ingredients for a meal.

"How bad do you want it?" he teased as he climbed over her body.

She'd never tire of touching him. Every time they connected, the mating touch would spark against her skin, sending goosebumps all over her flesh. His hair, his short beard that she'd asked him to keep, and the strength in his touch caused her to melt in his hands…or under his tongue in most cases.

His cock touched her opening, and Anna Claire raised her hips enough for him to slide inside her. As he seated himself, she felt the stirrings of release, but she didn't want it to end so soon. Clamping down on her desire, she rotated her hips to feel him deep in her core.

"Come here, honey," he breathed as he slid his arm under her body, sitting up so she was upright with him. They were face to face as he lifted her, slowly moving her small body up and down on his cock. "I want to watch you fall apart in my arms."

"Keep doing that," she hummed. "But I don't want it to end."

"You holding out on me?" he smirked. Anna Claire knew he was accepting her challenge by the growl and flash of fang he gave her.

"Never," she lied and eyed the mating mark on his neck. She leaned forward and brushed his hair off his neck. He cursed loudly as she ran her tongue ever so slowly over the mark.

"You're killing me."

"I'm killing you?" she asked with wide eyes and a roll of her hips. "You're making it very hard for me to make this last."

"Oh, honey, I can last all night for you," he teased and leaned forward, pushing her back to the mattress. His thrust once…twice, then held himself deep. "This is just round one."

The male of her dreams sent her over the edge within the next thirty seconds, making her attempt at lasting longer look weak. He didn't find his release, but thankfully, she was up for another romp beneath the sheets.

Flipping her over, he placed his hand over her belly where their cub rested in her womb. With his other hand, he pulled on her hips, putting her in the position of their mating. The moment he entered, Anna Claire felt another release brewing.

It was going to be a long night.

Chapter 10

Gunnar released his mate as soon as her climax subsided, but his hands weren't off her long. Her scent was all over the room, and his beast approved with a nudge inside his mind. Anna Claire stilled as her breathing slowed. He rearranged them so he could snuggle up behind his mate.

"What did you say about lasting longer?" he teased.

"You proved me wrong," she laughed, looking over at the clock. "It's been three hours."

"Not long enough, if you ask me," he replied as he buried his face in her long, blonde hair. Gods, her body was addictive. His beast rumbled inside as they both relaxed. The scent of sex mingled in the air with her pregnancy scent, and the freak in Gunnar wanted to wallow all over her to keep that on his skin. He wanted her mark and scent to be noticed by every female he ever crossed paths with, because he wanted everyone to know he belonged to Anna Claire.

They showered and eventually made their way back to the main house where Ada and Tessa were in the front living room, sitting on the floor with their cubs. Thane wasn't quite old enough to play with his cousin, Aria, but Ada had him laid out on a blanket next to the older child. Aria played with a stuffed toy while Thane practiced rolling over to his little belly.

Gunnar released Anna Claire and was about to ask where his brothers were when he saw them standing outside on the front porch with rifles in hand. He excused himself to head out the door, coming to Drake's side.

"Any news?" Gunnar used his bear's heightened senses to listen for anything out of the ordinary. With his vision, he scanned the front yard, thankful most of the trees that dotted the front part of their land worked to keep the house shielded from any gunfire. The only spot they had to be wary of was the driveway and barn. If those hunters set up in the same location again, they would easily be able to take out any of the clan if they were working on equipment.

With that revelation, the Morgan brothers had moved all of their plows and farming equipment to an old storage building that sat at the back of one of their fields. It was used by their father, and it wasn't sturdy enough to be safe, but at the moment, it was all they had.

"Nothing," Drake growled. "The sheriff is bringing the healer over today. I'm hoping that lawman is coming with more news."

"Gaia is coming, too," Rex added, causing Gunnar to raise a brow in his middle brother's direction.

"So, she's been hanging around Garrett a lot," he

observed. He'd never seen Gaia with a male, and he wasn't so sure he felt comfortable with their mother's friend getting mixed up with that angel.

"He better not lay a hand on her," Drake growled. The protectiveness to his words caused a rumble to go through Rex and Gunnar as well.

"They're here," Gunnar interrupted. "Let's take care of these hunters first. After that, we can run off the sheriff before he gets too close to Gaia."

The brothers nodded in agreement. He'd watch that sheriff and make sure he wasn't showing any feelings toward Gaia. Hell, Gunnar wasn't even sure the lawman could take a mate. He knew Gaia was made entirely different than the shifters. She was in human form, and after the shooting at her diner, they knew she couldn't heal like them. He didn't know if Sheriff Lynch had touched her or if she would be like the shifters and know when she touched her forever mate.

Did Mother Nature even have the ability to take on a mate?

Shaking his head, he decided to leave that question alone. Although Gaia wasn't connected to the gods, she had her own reasons for coming to Earth to care for her creations, and Gunnar doubted her job here had anything to do with finding a mate.

The brothers stepped off the porch the moment Garrett stopped his patrol car. The wind picked up his scent as the angel stepped out of his car. There was a hint of something sweet coming from Gaia as she exited the passenger side. An old pickup truck pulled in a few seconds later, and Gunnar relaxed when he recognized the panther's healer behind the wheel.

"Sheriff…Healer," Drake nodded to the males before turning for their friend. Drake frowned as he addressed Gaia. "Gaia."

"Drake," she replied, but his name sounded more like a question than a greeting when it rolled off her tongue.

"Let's go inside so we can make a plan," Rex offered.

"I'm here to check on Anna Claire," Harold began. "I will take my leave as soon as we are done."

"That would be wise," Drake rumbled as he turned for the door.

Gunnar waited for everyone to go ahead of him, stepping to the healer's side as he approached. "Sorry, it's been stressful around here."

"I know your clan doesn't like to ask for help, but we are always a call away should you need a little backup." Harold wasn't a threat to the Morgan clan, and even though they were weary of anyone who wasn't a part of their tight family, Gunnar felt at ease when the panther was there. It could've been simply because the male was a doctor and had offered his services to the females when they were with young and never caused problems when he was there. The male treated their females with great respect, and

Gunnar found he liked the cat a little more each time they interacted.

"How about that cup of coffee Anna Claire offered you the last time you came by?" Gunnar noticed how his mate enjoyed talking to the healer, and he would try to keep his paranoia to himself when he was visiting for her checkups.

But if the male did anything to harm his mate or anyone on their lands, the healer wouldn't be alive long enough to give himself aide.

Anna Claire sat up straighter when the door to their quarters opened to reveal her mate and the panther's healer. Harold smiled warmly as he entered, setting his black bag on the table by the door.

"How are you feeling, Anna Claire?"

"Much better," she promised, pointing to the recliner to her left. "Have a seat, healer. May I get you anything?"

"Your mate has offered me a cup of coffee," he announced with a smile. Gunnar was at the small kitchenette, pouring water into the coffee pot. When she cut her gaze toward the healer, the male just shrugged and pulled a stethoscope out of the pocket of his white coat. "Are you ready for your checkup?

We can chat over coffee after we check on your cub."

"Sure," she beamed.

"Are you still nauseous?" he asked.

"No," she replied. She felt heat on her cheeks as she remembered Gunnar hand feeding her crackers that first week. "My mate is a very good cook, and he's kept me well fed."

"That's good." Harold nodded as he made notes on a small spiral book he'd produced from his other pocket. "I'd like to listen to your cub's heartbeat."

"We can do that in the bedroom," she offered and stood. So far, the visits were all the same. He'd ask her questions and listen to the heartbeat while she lay on the bed. After he measured her growing belly, he would excuse himself and leave with a promise to come by in a month.

Gunnar followed them and stood protectively on the other side of the bed as she raised her shirt, tucking the ends in the elastic of her bra. The healer handed over a rag to cover her leggings. "This gel might be a little cool. I'm sorry."

"It's not that bad," she laughed as he squeezed the tube, making a spot of goo about the size of a half-dollar beside her belly button. The little hand-held wand touched her skin, and he moved it around until the whooshing sound of their cub's heart came from the speaker on a box he held in his other hand.

The healer did a few more measurements and tucked away his belongings in his worn medical bag.

"Everything sounds great. I would like to schedule a time for you to come by the pride to do an ultrasound in about a month."

A rumble built in Gunnar's throat, and Anna Claire narrowed her eyes on him. "I think that would be fine. You can put us down on your books for the twenty-fifth at ten in the morning."

"Sounds great," Harold replied, ignoring the glare from her mate.

"How about that cup of coffee?" she asked as she righted her clothes and came to her feet.

Harold looked a little weary with Gunnar following them quietly, but Anna Claire liked the panther. He was one of the kindest, most gentle males she'd ever met. Despite the Morgans' adversity to anyone not in their inner circle, she knew he wouldn't bring harm to the clan.

"How do you take your coffee?" she asked as she poured three cups.

"Black is fine," Harold said with a shake of his head. Gunnar finally relaxed as he took a seat on the couch. She handed over his coffee and set the healer's down on the side table for the male to pick up on his own since he'd already discarded the gloves he'd used when working with mated females.

Gunnar's eyes were the brown of his human side, and she breathed a sigh of relief when there was no presence of his beast. "How are you and your mate?"

"We have been quite busy, but I have an intern

now. He's going to assist me and take some of the weight off my back." Harold paused to take a sip of coffee. "I guess you've heard the Guardians are working with the human government?"

"What?" Gunnar asked, his eyes narrowing again. "We haven't heard anything."

"The FBI has hired the Guardians to help police the species." He frowned. "There are rogue shifters being controlled by some really bad alphas, and they've taken to terrorizing the humans."

"Oh, my gods," Anna Claire gasped, covering her mouth from the news. "We have been in hibernation for the past few months."

"They are staying up in the Memphis area," he confirmed. "So far, they've captured several wolf shifters and sent them to a pride in Colorado to be reformed, I guess you could say. It's nothing for your species to worry about, though. With the grizzly's differences, you have nothing to worry about."

Anna Claire's kind didn't need an alpha, but other species did. Hearing there were rogue alphas out there sent a chill of fear up her spine. She wasn't worried about herself…she was worried for them.

"I wish there was something we could do," she replied, sadness coating her words.

"We have it covered, but there is a war out there that we must fight to keep the humans and our pride safe. These rogues are turning females to fight against our Guardians. The alphas know we won't harm a female of any species, and it's taken a toll on our males."

"I've heard your pride allows females to protect you," Anna Claire blurted. It was the perfect time to ask him about the rumors. "Is that true?"

"Yes," he nodded, but the smile he gave her was one full of pride. "They have trained with the Guardians, and we have three females who are on rotation to help round up the rogue females. They have done well in finding them, too."

"That's just one more thing we need to worry about," Gunnar mumbled from his post beside her. He'd been mostly quiet, but the news of danger close to home had him sitting forward and, from the mating scent coming from his skin, she knew he was thinking about her safety.

"One more thing?" Harold questioned.

Gunnar quieted, and she could tell he was weighing his words, unsure if he should tell the healer what was going on with their clan.

"We've had problems of our own," Gunnar finally replied.

He launched into the information they had with the human hunters, promising it was only the bear shifters they were after. He'd mentioned the sheriff's vision. Harold's eyes sparkled with the amber flecks of his beast as her mate gave him the information.

"I know we are at war, and I understand your clan's secrecy, but you know we will help you with anything regarding a threat." Harold shook his head in disgust and drained the rest of his coffee. When he stood, Gunnar followed and accepted the handshake the male offered. "Please call us if you need anything, Gunnar."

"We appreciate your offer," he replied, but didn't give Harold a definite answer.

Anna Claire smiled warmly at the healer and promised to come by for her ultrasound in a month. She was happy he'd stayed and given them a moment to talk. Gunnar was a little more at ease with the male even though he had brought some disturbing news.

Maybe she could help bridge the gap in friendship between her clan and the healer's pride. It was important now more than ever that they stick together. Their species was being attacked, and they needed to work as allies and finally, after all this time, make a pact to become friends.

Chapter 11

Harvey smirked as the offers for help arrived in his email. Three more hunters were on their way to help with the efforts to eradicate the clan of bear shifters. They had two days until the first, and it was time to sneak out to their lands to count heads, so to speak.

"When the others get here, we will head out," he announced to the two males who'd taken up residence in his home over the past week. "I have enough supplies for everyone to cover their scent, too."

Harvey held up a few bottles of spray and placed them on the table along with several camouflaged hats, jackets, and pants.

"Deer spray?" Don frowned as he picked up the bottles and read the labels. "You sure this will work?"

"It covers your scent," Harvey scoffed. "Of course, it'll work."

"But the message boards said they have some super sensitive noses," he responded, picking up a cloth mask before tossing it back on the table. He reached for the beanie hat and tucked it in his pocket.

"So do deer," Harvey said with a nod. That damn kid had questioned a lot of things since his arrival, and Harvey wished his father would take that boy in hand.

Skipper found a camo jacket in the pile and tried it on for fit. Once he was satisfied, he walked over to the couch and took a seat. "The scent spray isn't guaranteed, but wouldn't you want to have it just in case it does work?"

"True," Don nodded.

A car pulled into his driveway, and Harvey left the father and son to greet the three males who'd come from Arkansas. They were already decked out in their fatigues as they exited the vehicle.

"Larry, Bruce, Elvin," Harvey greeted. The males were all in their mid to late forties and wore scruffy beards. "Come on inside and meet the others."

Once everyone finished mingling and making introductions, Harvey checked the clock. "We need to leave."

He'd already sent the new arrivals the aerial map of the clan's land. They'd come in from the southeast and make their way through the land, coming up behind the three cabins in the woods. The main house would have to be scoped out with binoculars from a spot away from the trails the bears had made through the wooded lot. The only trail leading to the main home went directly past the cabins. If they attempted to go through the denser part of the woods, they were sure to make too much noise.

Anna Claire watched as the sun set on another perfect day. Unfortunately, she couldn't sit on the front porch to do so. The couch in the main living room faced the window to the west, and she'd cracked the blinds just enough to soak in the last rays of the day.

Occasionally, a car would pass on the road, but other than that, everything was quiet. She'd always wondered what her life would have been like if she'd been human. They were weird creatures, and from what she'd seen online, they were nothing like the bears. The news reports showed so much violence between them. Not that the shifters weren't violent, but at least when her kind were violent, there was a reason. Humans were greedy.

"You okay out here?" Ada asked as she joined her on the couch. Her cub, Thane, slept peacefully in her arms.

"Yeah," Anna Claire nodded. "Just daydreaming."

"About?"

"Nothing really," she shrugged. "I'm worried about the hunters coming here."

"The males have a plan, and so do we," Ada reassured her.

The sheriff had been coming around a lot, and she'd noticed how Drake, Rex, and Gunnar were starting to trust him more. She wanted to snicker. The male wasn't as conniving as the brothers thought. Somewhere, deep down behind his wall of protection for those panthers, the male was still an angel sent from the gods.

He was tasked to help the cats, not the bears. But when he had visions, he was adamant about sharing the information. She wasn't going to deny his suggestions about precautions, either.

"We should listen to the sheriff more," Anna Claire began. "I hate that the brothers are so reluctant to accept help or even become friends with him or the panthers."

"The Shaw pride has done nothing to harm the Morgan clan," Ada agreed with a heavy sigh. "They've proved their friendship and loyalty many times over."

"They saved us," Anna Claire reminded her friend. "We would've been in a really bad place if you hadn't escaped and come here."

"I had no idea I was even on a grizzly's land," Ada reminded her. "I was cold and needed to bed down for the winter."

"Someone, somewhere, sent you here," she replied.

"Probably Gaia," Ada chuckled.

"Probably," Anna Claire smirked before both of

them started laughing.

The two friends stopped for a moment as they calmed. Ada reached for Anna Claire's hand and gave it a little squeeze. "How's the cub?"

"It's perfectly fine and growing as expected," Anna Claire beamed.

"You look so happy," Ada observed.

"I am…I really am." Anna Claire wasn't lying. Gunnar had been everything she'd ever wanted in a mate. She loved him. Hell, she'd loved him from the time she'd been rescued, but it took almost a year's worth of friendship and healing to complete them.

"He's good for you."

"I think so," Anna Claire agreed.

"How are you dealing with…" Ada gave her a serious look, and she knew exactly what her friend was asking.

"They didn't penetrate me." She paused to swallow a lump in her throat. "They touched me inappropriately, though." She shivered and tightened her fists that rested over her small baby bump.

"How did Gunnar take the news?"

"Not well at first," Anna Claire replied. "He was angry, but he kept his temper in check around me. I saw his beast in his eyes, though."

"Are you having any reservations?" Ada had been her best friend and a confidant when they were living in the O'Kelly clan. There wasn't anything she couldn't say to the female. They'd both been through so much.

"No, not at all." Anna Claire sighed and shifted in her seat to turn toward her friend. "With Gunnar, all of that just went away after a while. He was my friend before he was my mate. It took me a long time to tell him what had happened, but when I did, it was like lifting a weight from my mind and body. Once we finally touched and mated, I just let it all go."

"He really is perfect for you," Ada said, using her free arm to hug Anna Claire.

"He is," she replied with a wide smile.

They quieted as they heard Gunnar's truck arrive. He'd been working in the fields all day. The females were being watched over, but for the last hour, Luca had been working at the elder's home finishing up the underground shelter below their cabins. The first of the month was only a day away, and they needed to get everything prepared.

"I'll head back to put him down so you can have a few moments with your mate," Ada offered, nodding to Gunnar as he entered the living room.

"Good evening," Gunnar said as he leaned over to kiss his mate. The magic that connected them swirled around her body, and she felt a need deep in her core. "You smell amazing."

"So do you," she teased as his mating scent reached her nose.

"Come to our room," he ordered. "I want to spend some time with you before I have to start dinner."

Anna Claire took his hand and let her mate take them back to their quarters where they got lost in each other for the next hour and a half.

Dinner was going to be a little late that night.

Gunnar kissed his mate for probably the hundredth time since he'd arrived home. He couldn't get enough of her body or scent. It was almost seven before he finally broke away to head to the main house to make a quick meal. She promised to be there after she showered, and he had to force himself away from their room when she padded naked from the bed to the bathroom to start the water.

Up in the main house, Drake and Rex were coming in from the fields. Everything was planted, but with the absence of rain over the last few days, they'd set up the watering system to care for the seeds as they began to sprout.

"After dinner, I think it would be best if we check the property," Drake announced as he took a seat at the head of the table.

"That would be a good idea," Gunnar replied as he stirred the pot of chili. "I'll go with you."

"We need one more, because I have to work on

some small engine equipment that I've been neglecting," Rex said. "I'll call Ransom to see if he's free."

Rex walked out of the room to place the call. Gunnar looked up as his mate entered the kitchen with her small hand resting casually on her stomach. He still couldn't believe he was going to be a father.

When the time came, during the winter while they were in hibernation, he would take the reins and deliver his cub just as his brothers had done and his father before him. It was tradition and something all males taught their sons when they were old enough to find their own mates.

"That looks amazing," she hummed as he ladled a bowl for her, adding a pinch of shredded cheese to the top. "You remembered?"

"I remember everything about you," he replied before taking the bowl to the table. He remembered how she'd asked for cheese with her chili with fear in her eyes the first time he'd made it. He swore to himself that he would never let her go a day without for the rest of her life, and he'd hoped he'd kept that promise so far.

After he was satisfied she was eating, he made himself a bowl and sat to her left. Drake and Tessa were quiet as they ate their meal while their cub ate some meat Gunnar had pulled out from the mass he'd cooked to add to his meal.

"Do you think they've been back?" Anna Claire

asked as her hand went suddenly still. The spoon was halfway to her mouth, and a bit of the liquid dripped back into her bowl. "I mean, shouldn't you take more than just three of you to check?"

"We know there is at least three of them," Gunnar replied, taking her free hand with his own. She dropped the spoon in the bowl and pulled her hand free. He'd noticed how she did that whenever she was worried or about to panic.

"What do you want us to do should they be out in the woods?" She was thinking hard about the hunters, and it killed Gunnar to know she was feeling anything other than peace and safety, but she was right…they had all their plans in place except one.

"Call the sheriff," Drake grunted as he took another bite of his meal. "As much as I don't like having that angel here, he would be the best person to call. He could be here in a second with that disappearing act he does."

Gunnar caught a bright smile coming from his mate. She'd been placing little hints around about how much she liked the panther's healer and the angel, and how she wished they would at least try to be friends with the other shifters in the area.

Again, his mate was right.

"It's better to have the cats here if they are available," Gunnar offered, looking dead into his brother's eyes. He saw the resistance, but he also saw a glimmer of hope there, too. Grumpy ole Drake was coming around.

"I'll program the sheriff's number into the mates' phones," Rex offered. "I will be close if anything happens on your run tonight, anyway. I doubt we will need anyone to come help us, but Drake is right. If you have your phones on you, please put them on the table."

Rex knew not to touch the females or take anything from their hands. Tessa, Ada, and Anna Claire pulled their phones from their pockets and slid them to the middle of the table. Rex took each one and programed in the numbers. His long hair fell forward as he worked, and Gunnar could see the tight set to his shoulders. The male was as concerned as everyone else.

"If there is a problem, everyone goes to their quarters and locks the doors. Call the sheriff and wait," Rex ordered, handing his mate's phone over and setting the other two in the middle of the table where they had been placed before.

Anna Claire took her phone and found the entry, nodding when she agreed to do as Gunnar's brother had ordered. Tessa did the same and the house fell silent as they finished their meal. Once Rex and Drake cleaned everything up, Gunnar stood from his seat.

"We won't be gone long," he promised and leaned over to kiss his mate. He inhaled her scent and took that with him as he and Drake stepped out onto the back porch to see Ransom arriving in his already shifted form.

He glanced over his shoulder and saw his mate standing there, biting her bottom lip. It was another one of her nervous tics, and he made a motion to shoo her away from the door. She knew he wanted the blinds closed and did so with no hesitation.

"Shift and let's hunt," Drake said, removing his shirt.

Gunnar did the same and let his animal free. The change was over in a few seconds, and his beast stepped off the porch, ready to hunt for the humans and protect his clan.

Rex exited the house and used his key to lock the deadbolt. He nodded toward the bears and took off on foot to the barn. Gunnar, Drake, and Ransom followed him to ensure his safe arrival. The bears nervously looked over their left shoulders at the road in front of their land, expecting to hear a shot ring out into the night, but it never came.

As their animals relaxed, the human part of their mind was on alert. The bears were deadly, but they were also ruled by their nature. Killing anything that moved was an easy task when you let the wild part of your animal loose. In the old days, they would let their beasts rule, but now, with the humans knowing about them, Gunnar had to keep his animal on a leash. They couldn't dole out punishment like they'd done with the others. The sheriff would get involved if they came back.

The beast growled low in his throat at the thought of not having an enemy's blood on his tongue. *Easy now.*

The animals knew the lands well. They'd even marked trees by scratching them with their claws during some of their runs. It was part of marking their territory, and it was a sign to other males in the area that there were mated females close. If they were smart, they'd turn around and leave immediately.

The night was warmer than it'd been that spring. Gunnar's bear scented the ground and was pleased to find only those of his clan had passed over the road leading to the new cabins. Drake's beast wandered over to the elder's homes, while Gunnar checked for foreign scents around Ransom and Luca's place. He was sure they'd already done that, but he wanted to make sure.

Once the homes were cleared, Drake's bear huffed and tossed its head toward the woods and the opening of the trail they used to access the wooded area of their land. Gunnar followed beside his brother and let the bear have full rein for a while. It was time to hunt, and with one last push to his beast, Gunnar let the animal roam, hoping he didn't find anything in his search.

Chapter 12

Gaia sat at her kitchen table, picking at the food she'd made with fresh ingredients from her little greenhouse in the backyard. Something wasn't right, and she was worried for her bears. The last thing she'd heard from them was to lay low and let them find those hunters.

The sheriff had a patrol car come by once or twice every hour to check on her home. The persons responsible for shooting up her diner hadn't been found, and that worried her. If they knew she was involved with the bears, would she be able to stay?

As much as she wanted to protect them, protecting herself from a human death was at the top of her priority list. If she died, all of them would follow. She was the air they breathed and the soil in which they grew their food. Gaia provided them with the water they needed to keep their bodies alive, too.

There was so much she was involved in to keep the human population alive, but without her, they would have nothing. She'd never wanted for herself, knowing she was the one responsible to keep the circle of life going.

In her millions of years, she'd seen what the gods had done. It was Gaia who'd caused the floods and droughts over the course of time. The Ice Age was a disaster, and the gods had angered her when they had made the dinosaurs. She originally let them do their thing, but after a while, the path of the dinosaurs came to a point where those animals had to go. They were nothing but a design flaw, and to be honest, they were too damn destructive. She'd brought forth the volcanic eruptions after a few asteroids hit the earth, and in a matter of time, they were all gone.

The beginning of modern times came with it the need to live off the land. Once humans were put on earth, things changed for the better. She was able to give them the tools to live, and in the beginning, they thrived, growing to massive numbers.

The shifters were made by the gods, and while she didn't disagree with their creation, she did hate that they were placed here amongst the humans who lived in fear of anything that could kill them.

Now, they were known, and with that information, some of the humans had come out as mercenaries, vowing to kill off the shifter population. And that population included her bears. If she could just find the male responsible for starting it, she would gladly put an end to his plans.

Grabbing her computer, she did something she said she'd never do. Accessing the dark web was tricky, but at that point, she didn't care. The males had told her what they had found, but she wanted to see it for herself.

A few clicks and a general search for shifters later, she found what she was looking for, only to be scared out of her mind when someone knocked on the front door.

She jumped from her seat and ran toward the door where Drake had left one of his extra shotguns. His father had taught her long ago how to handle the weapon regardless of her own abilities. She may not have been the cleanest shot, but she knew how to aim for the center of a human and make them regret it. With the gun in her hand, she peeked through the hole in the door, deflating when she saw it was the sheriff.

"What are you doing here?" Her voice was a little angrier than he'd probably ever heard from her, and that was evident when he took a half-step back.

"Checking on you." He frowned and adjusted his bulletproof vest behind his uniform shirt. She wanted to chuckle because she doubted the male could be killed with human weapons. He was already dead, wasn't he? "What's going on, Gaia?"

"Nothing," she blurted as she remembered having the dark web still pulled up on her computer. The last thing she needed was Garrett seeing her snooping.

"It doesn't seem like nothing," Garrett pressed. The male was a cop in his human life. She should know better than to lie to him, but she didn't want to be caught. "Can I come in? We can talk about what's bothering you."

"I'm fine, really, Garrett," she said, relaxing her shoulders. "You really did scare me."

"Everyone is on edge," he replied and looked over his shoulder. He narrowed his gaze and tucked his chin, saying her name like a curse.

"Garrett, wait!" she begged, but it was no use. The male pushed past her and walked over toward her small desk where the computer was sitting. She cursed under her breath and followed him inside after closing and locking the door. "I can explain."

"You better start explaining then," he warned. "I have too many people accessing this website in my town, and if it keeps going, the feds will be here. As you know, I don't have time for any of that to come my way."

"I need to know what is going on," she sighed. The expulsion of breath was one of frustration. "Explain all of this to me."

Gaia pointed to the screen where a new post had been made. The person writing it had a fake name that simply marked him as "Hacker01".

We are a day away from D-Day. We want to find them in their animal form, and when you make sure they aren't breathing anymore, post pictures of their bodies.

"Why would they want to do that?" she cried, feeling tears prick at her emerald eyes.

"They want fame," Garrett answered with a soft voice. He placed his hand on her shoulder, and the comfort was welcomed. "We've found several tabloids who are willing to pay millions for images of deceased shifters."

"Millions?" she gasped as she spun around to face him. The angel grasped her shoulders to steady her when she swayed. "We can't let this happen, Garrett. We just can't let them hurt the bears."

"We have been keeping an eye on their lands," he promised, releasing his hold. She wanted to reach out for him, but instead, she dropped to the office chair behind her. "Drake and the others are prepared."

"What can I do?" she begged, needing to do something. She'd promised to protect them at all costs, but this was something she was unable to stop.

"You need to keep yourself safe," he ordered, kneeling before her. When he took her chin with his crooked finger, she stared into his eyes…his real ones. They were completely white. The angel was having a hard time with the news, as well. "They already know about you, too. My assumption is they think you are a shifter."

"I need to know when exactly they will strike," she said through gritted teeth. There was a storm brewing inside her, and she wanted to use that to wipe out those hunters.

"What are you planning?" he asked, narrowing his eyes as he searched her face for any information.

"Nothing that will harm the town," she vowed.

Gunnar's beast was on edge, scenting every inch of the forest behind his home. His brother, Drake, and Ransom O'Kelly were doing the same several yards away. They'd checked the denser part of the woods leading to the back of their property line to find nothing of interest just as the sun was setting two days before the sheriff's vision was to come for them.

Gunnar turned to the west, planning on checking the trails, when he heard a branch snap in the direction he was heading. The others were behind him, and he knew no one would be as stupid as to be snooping around their property shortly after nightfall.

His beast quieted, hoping the other bears had heard the noise as well. He scented the air and waited for the wind to change, blowing the scent of humans in his face.

There were six male scents, but they were a little…off. There was some chemical on their clothes, and it only took him a second to realize they'd sprayed themselves with the chemical hunters used when tracking deer during their hunting season.

Gods, he wanted to roll his eyes so bad. Those idiots were going to get themselves killed.

Ransom and Drake were quiet as they approached. As large as they were, they'd learned to keep their sounds to a minimum when hunting for their food. This time, they weren't looking for food, they were going to find and eliminate the threat to the clan.

Gunnar wanted to shift, but he couldn't risk being seen or heard when he told the other males his plan. They'd have to go off on their own since they couldn't communicate between themselves other than a few head jerks and huffs to voice their displeasure.

They froze at the sound of the humans speaking. Gunnar calmed his breathing as he listened.

"Stay to the trails," an older male said. "They're not even going to know we are here."

"You better hope this deer spray works," a younger male sneered.

Gunnar wanted to laugh and shift anyway just to tell them that it did not work, but he kept his animal form and took a step.

Off in the distance, he saw movement, and from the soft growl coming from his brother, Gunnar knew he'd seen them, too. Six human males carried shotguns and were dressed head to toe in camo. They didn't do much to cover their faces, so their skin stuck out like a sore thumb.

He knew he couldn't call for backup, but from the looks of it, they weren't going to need it. Those hunters were not as skilled as they'd all believed. It would be better to just capture them and hand them over to Garrett instead of killing them.

"Look for their bitches," another one whispered. "We can save them before these bastards knock 'em up with their spawn."

Okay, Gunnar had decided to kill them.

Once they spoke of the mates, he knew they would need to be put down like a feral shifter. The guns they carried gave them a little advantage, but that was it.

"Harvey?" another one whispered. "What do they look like in their human form?"

"Does it matter?" Harvey replied. That was the male the sheriff had been looking for from the chat rooms. He was the one responsible for shooting at Gunnar's mate. "We are on their land, and if they are out in these woods, or come outside of those homes, we kill them."

When he turned to look at his brother's beast, it lowered its head to the ground for a second to acknowledge Gunnar's right to end his life. Shifter law had been around since the beginning, and every male knew to let the rightful mate take the life of a threat.

The males waited for the humans to come near. Their footsteps sounded as they reached the main trail. At that point, the bears could see them as they approached. There had never been this easy of a kill.

Thunder rumbled off in the distance a few seconds after a flash of lighting lit up the sky. Fortunately, the hunters didn't see the bears waiting patiently beside the trail. They'd all turned to look behind them at the flash. Gunnar was sure Gaia had something to do with that.

They were about fifty yards away and coming closer at a snail's pace. Gunnar's bear wanted to rush them, but he held back. With the guns, he had to proceed with caution.

He glanced at Drake's bear. It was rocking forward and back as if Drake was holding back his beast, too. Ransom was as still as the night, but that didn't mean the male was unprepared.

A branch cracked as the youngest male came up beside a male who looked like his father. The kid searched through the darkness, only relying on his human vision…which wasn't anything extraordinary.

"Their cabins are not far," Harvey whispered to the others.

Another louder boom of thunder rumbled the area as the males came to a halt only feet from the bears. They still hadn't been seen, but that was quickly going to change. Gunnar had it out for the leader of the group, and he was poised to take him down.

Drake broke the silence as one of them raised their gun to look through a scope. The gasp from the middle-aged male sent them into action. There was no time to call out a warning before Drake stood on his hind legs and swiped the shotgun from the male's grasp.

A shot rang out, but Gunnar heard the bullet thud into a tree somewhere to his right. His bear rushed the male who'd shot his mate, taking him to the ground.

"No, please!" Harvey begged for his life, but there would be no mercy here. They'd tried to kill them, and when his mate was shot, shifter law had been activated.

The sheriff wasn't there to stop him as his beast pressed the male into the ground with his large paw, raking his abdomen with his sharp claws.

This is for my mate, you son of a bitch!

Harvey's life spilled out onto the ground as his brother and Ransom were going after the others. Another shot went off, and Anna Claire's cousin roared at the impact. He was hit right behind his left shoulder. The wound could be fatal, but there was no time to get the male to shift.

Gunnar launched himself at the middle-aged man, taking him to the ground as well. Drake howled as a bullet hit him from the younger human, but it didn't stop him. Two more human males took off at a dead run toward the back of their property. Gunnar's bear insisted he follow, but he had to take care of the one underneath him. With swift movements, he bit into the male's throat and ended his miserable life.

He had to leave Ransom in the woods while Drake took care of the other two humans. There were six in all, and that should've been an easy takedown, but with the guns involved, the odds were in the humans' favor. He needed to find the other two who had gotten away, but he also needed to get Ransom medical help.

Anna Claire jumped from her seat as she heard the sound of gunshots off in the distance. Ada and Tessa were already scooping up their cubs as Rex burst through the doors.

"Everyone in their quarters, now!" Luca ordered as Rex grabbed for weapons. Their eyes shifted to account for the now darkened sky. It was only after eight, and she wondered why the hunters were so careless as to be on their land so early.

"Rex!" Ada cried out as she bundled Thane against her chest.

"Ada, go now! I mean it!" he ordered, throwing the blinds and bar across the front door.

Anna Claire hurried to her room and barred the door, reaching for her cell phone. Her first call was to the sheriff, and she cursed when he didn't answer right away. One more attempt to call and he answered right away.

"Sheriff Lynch," he bellowed into the phone.

"Garrett, it's Anna Claire," she cried. "Someone is on our land, and I hear gunshots. Send help, please!"

She wasn't above begging, and the tears were coming faster as she fretted over the status of her mate. Was he shot? Did they catch the humans yet? Was everyone going to be safe, or were they sitting ducks in their underground bunkers?

"I'll be there in a flash," he promised. "Where are they?"

"Drake, Gunnar, and Ransom went out to search the land after dinner. They'd only been gone maybe thirty minutes before the gunshots started. Please, sheriff…hurry!"

"Get to your safe rooms and don't come out until you hear from me or your mates," he ordered. "Do you understand? Anna Claire?"

"Yes, yes! We are already inside," she promised. "Hurry."

The line disconnected and she sat heavily on the bed, wiping tears away from her eyes so she could see to dial one of the other mates. As she covered her unborn cub with her hand, she called Tessa to make sure she was okay. "Three-way call Ada."

Thankfully, the females had shown her how to do it on the cell phone Gunnar had given her. She wished they had some way of seeing what the hell was going on outside on the lands.

"Ada? Are you okay?" she asked into the phone the moment the female answered. Anna Claire could hear her cub crying, and she knew Ada needed to calm down for her young. "Breathe. We are safe right now, and I called the sheriff. He's on the way."

"Thank the gods," Ada gasped. "Why did those hunters come so early?"

"I don't know," Anna Claire replied.

"They were probably checking out our paths and figuring a way into the compound," Tessa growled. "I told Drake we needed to get cameras!"

"It's too late now to get angry about what we should've done," Ada reminded them. "We thought we were safe from the humans hunting us, but now we know that they are smarter than we gave them credit for."

"We need to find the hacker and put a stop to this," Anna Claire said through gritted teeth. "He's the one who started this mess, and when he is located, I want to know how he found out about us."

"Let me grab the burner phone," Tessa offered. "I can do some snooping."

"Hurry," Ada said in a rush.

"Everyone come to my quarters," Anna Claire suggested.

Her next call was to the elders. They were holed up in their new basements. They assured her everything was fine and they had enough supplies. She reminded them to stay locked in and someone would come get them when it was all over.

She prayed everyone was going to be okay, but she had a bad feeling something was going to happen to change their very existence.

Chapter 13

"Son of a bitch!" Sheriff Lynch barked as his eyes turned bright white. His arm shot out and reached for Gaia, pushing her behind his back for protection. "It's already started."

"What's started?" she asked, pulling on his arm. "The mass killing?"

He gave her the rundown of what Anna Claire had rambled into the phone when he'd finally answered. Gaia's eyes started to swirl, but Garrett didn't have time to calm her down. "Stay here and don't you dare leave. Do you understand me?"

"I'm coming with you," she demanded, and held out her hands, producing glowing orbs of flames. "Don't try and stop me either, sheriff."

They'd been talking more about the dark web, and she'd asked him to stay for dinner. Garrett knew he should've left before then, but he just didn't care to leave. He didn't want to leave the female for fear of someone coming to her home. Little did he know, it was the hunters who would jump the gun and head for the clan.

"You can't follow me," he retorted, knowing she couldn't teleport like him. "It's not safe. I have to go."

And just like that, he focused on the Morgans' land and let his magic take him to the woods behind the bear's home. He heard them running through the woods, not caring they were making noise. He closed his eyes and reformed deeper into the clan's land, holding up his hands when two bears skidded to a halt in front of him.

"What's going on?" Garrett barked. He couldn't communicate with them or even tell them apart, but when one of them shimmered and formed into the youngest Morgan brother, he knew something was terribly wrong.

"Two males escaped," Gunnar panted. "They have guns, and Ransom was shot. We left him in the woods to go after the humans, but he needs medical assistance. He's been struck, and it looks like it could be fatal if someone doesn't go in there and take that fucking bullet out."

"Do you want me to call the healer?" Garrett confirmed.

"Yes!" Gunnar yelled, his face beginning to shift again. His nose elongated, and his canines grew thick in his mouth as fur began to form on his human skin. "Get Ransom to the pride, because it's too dangerous here."

Gunnar shifted again, and he ran in the direction his brother had passed only a moment before. Garrett closed his eyes and listened for Ransom, praying to the gods to give him the answers he needed.

A growl interrupted his prayer, and he looked up to see Luca and Rex barreling toward him. He quickly told them what Gunnar had said before he felt a shiver roll over his skin. The gods were angry.

"Where's Ransom?" Luca begged. "Where's my brother?"

"He's somewhere around here," Garrett said. "He's been shot, and I need to get him to the healer."

"Fuck," Rex barked as he spun around in a circle, lifting his partially shifted nose to the sky.

"If we can find him, I can transport him to the pride," Garrett promised, taking his phone from his pocket to place the call to Harold.

"Sheriff?" Harold answered. "What can I do for you?"

"Bears," Garrett panted as he ran. "Can you operate on them?"

"What's going on?" Harold asked, his voice changing to that of his calling. "Where are they?"

"Human hunters came early, and Ransom has been shot. He's somewhere in the woods behind their home. I'm searching for him now, and once I find him, I will zap him over to you."

"I'll be ready," Harold promised.

Luca called out for his brother, but there was no answer. Rex shifted to his bear form to use his heightened sense of smell. When the bear locked onto the scent, he turned to the south and ran down a pathway already cut into the wooded lot.

Luca's shout indicated they'd found the male, and when Garrett arrived, he found Ransom in his human form, naked and covered in his own blood. Beside him were the bodies of four males, all different ages.

"Leave the bodies," Garrett ordered. "I'll get him help and come back to take care of that."

Ransom moaned as he was lifted. There was no fight left in the male as Garrett called upon his heavenly senses and transported them to the front porch of the healer's home.

"He's not going to make it," Garrett cursed as the panther's healer jerked the door open wide. "Can you do something? Anything?"

"Take him in here," Harold said as he headed toward the back of his home. The small operating room was for his shifters. They usually didn't require much more than a few stitches, but the room was there, sanitized for emergencies.

The panther's healer had converted his old home into a medical facility many years before. He worked on the panthers and assisted in the births of the cubs all in that little room, but he had every tool imaginable to do the necessary work.

"If you're going to stay here, then move out of my way," Harold ordered.

"I have to help the Morgans find who did this," Garrett said, giving Harold a nod. "I'll be back."

"Be safe," the healer said as Garrett disappeared.

Once he arrived back at his first location, he stood over the bodies of the human males. The grizzlies hadn't been easy on them, and they'd had every right to do what they needed to get them away from their homes and mates.

With his hand held out in front of him, he closed his eyes and felt the power come through him. Heat developed in his hand much like Gaia did with her flames. Only his heat was more of a transfer of power from the gods. With a soft prayer, he waved his hand in a circle and waited for the brightness to die down. When he opened his eyes again, all the males and the evidence of their deaths was erased from the ground.

He hurried out of the woods and came upon the house where Gaia's white car was pulling into the drive. Anger built deep in his chest, and his eyes flashed white again. A wave of protectiveness came over the sheriff at seeing the female right in the heart of a war.

She glared at him as she exited. "Where are they?" Her voice wasn't kind. The female was beyond angry. Well, so was Garrett.

"I told you not to come here," he barked.

"I've never let a male tell me how to live my life, and I sure as hell am not going to start now."

"You are so damn stubborn!" he roared.

"Where is everyone?" Gaia ignored him and approached, never casting her swirling eyes away from his white ones. "We can do this the easy way or the hard one, Garrett."

"The females are inside, and Drake and Gunnar are on foot," he informed her with a heavy sigh. "Ransom is at the pride's healer having surgery to save his life."

He raised a brow when she cursed.

"You're in my way, sheriff," she observed, her eyes swirling faster.

"You shouldn't be here," he repeated.

"It's not your choice whether I come here or not. You don't have any rights to them!" she snarled, her hands glowing at her sides. The thunder rumbling around them became louder; lightning striking off in the distance. Rain rushed out of the clouds building above their heads, and he was powerless to stop her from causing so much destruction.

But he tried.

"Gaia, stop!" he yelled over the next clap of thunder. The two of them were almost nose to nose. Her eyes were swirling, and he was certain anything he said to her was going to be ignored. "You have to stop!"

"Get away from my bears!" she said as she shoved her hands forward. The balls of fire she'd produced smacked him in the chest, knocking the sheriff on his ass. He gasped for air to call out to her, but she stomped off toward the back of the house.

As he began to stand, a tingling of awareness registered in the back of his mind. The world around him faded as images rushed through his mind. The messages were like a film tripled in speed. *The bears…a death…females crying…and humans parading the corpses of the grizzly shifters through the streets.*

Anna Claire watched Tessa scrolling through the chat rooms, looking for any information on the hacker. She steadily wiped the tears from her eyes, worrying over her cousin. It was too dangerous to leave the house and head to the panther's land to be with Ransom. She had to trust in the healer's abilities to keep him alive.

"He's in great hands," Ada promised as she wrapped her arm around Anna Claire's shoulders. "All we can do now is wait and help find this hacker."

"I know," Anna Claire sniffled. "He's my blood. I can't lose another person in my life…I just can't." She thought of her mother and the tragic end to her life.

Anna Claire wanted to scream and throw things, but she knew it wouldn't help the fact that, yet again, someone had harmed a person she loved. Gunnar was out searching for more of the hunters, and fresh tears fell from her eyes when she thought of what could happen.

"Here, look!" Tessa set the phone down on the small table and pointed to a link she'd found in the hacker's profile. Clicking on it, the page was redirected to a website for a blogger. The blog was nothing more than an overabundance of conspiracy theories regarding the shifters, retail businesses, and one on a local government issue in Salt Lake City, Utah.

Tessa clicked it, and the hacker detailed several things only a person living there would know. The article was more a rant than anything, but at the end...they found something.

"He refers to the mayor's office as if he works there," Ada hummed.

"This guy works for the mayor, or *is* the mayor," Tessa corrected. "Holy shit."

"Does the sheriff know any of this?" Anna Claire asked, thankful they'd possibly found something.

"I don't know," Tessa shrugged. "I'm saving this information to give to Garrett."

A knock registered on the outer door and all three of them froze. Tessa reached for the shotgun Gunnar had left by their door and took a step back, pressing the stock of the weapon against her shoulder as if she'd done it a million times before.

Ada held her finger up to her lips, and Anna Claire prayed the cubs wouldn't wake from their naps. If the person on the other side of the door was human, the noise from a crying cub would alert them.

Anna Claire breathed slowly, coming to stand at Tessa's left side. Ada came to her right. Together, they would take out anyone who tried to come through the door. Her beast pushed at her skin, and for once, she let the grizzly partially shift with the anger she was feeling at being ambushed in her own home.

"Anna Claire!" the sheriff yelled from the other side of the door. "Are you in there?"

"Ada!" Rex hollered. "Open the door. It's okay."

Anna Claire knew the sheriff was on their side despite her mate's opinion of the male. Tapping Tessa on the shoulder, she waited for the female to lower the gun and reached for the metal bar across the door.

"Keep that shotgun handy." Anna Claire mumbled as she unlocked the first deadbolt.

The sheriff's eyes were as wide as saucers, but there was no color to them; only a ghostly white. Behind him, Gaia stood with her eyes swirling. "Gaia?"

"Where are the other males?" Sheriff Lynch growled.

"They're hunting the last two," Rex replied and walked over to his mate, leaning down to kiss his cub's tiny head to keep the male from being upset. He settled down once his father placed his large hand on his back and began rubbing him softly.

"I have to find them," Sheriff Lynch began,

cutting off Rex when he started to protest. "This is now my fight. I've had another vision."

A round of curses lit up the room, and Anna Claire felt fear race up her spine at the thought of what the angel had seen. "What have you seen?"

"I must go," the sheriff hedged. There was something he wasn't telling them, and Anna Claire knew it. She could scent it on him, and the smell burned her nose.

"We are okay here," Rex promised. "The house is secured, and we have guns." He nodded toward Tessa's weapon.

"I'll be back," the sheriff said, but his eyes fell on Gaia. "Stay here and don't leave. Once we find these assholes, I pray that it'll be over for this area."

"Stay safe," Rex said as he and the sheriff turned for the door.

"We have to help all of them," Ada gasped, but waved her hands in the air to stop the males from leaving. "We think we found who the hacker is."

"It's going to have to wait," he replied, walking away from the door. He stopped halfway up the hallway and called out over his shoulder. "Gaia, get inside and lock the door with the females. I'll get the information from you later…after this is all over."

"But…" Anna Claire called out, but it was too late. The sheriff disappeared into nothingness.

"Lock the door and let's wait it out," Tessa suggested, using her foot to close the reinforced door to Anna Claire's quarters.

Tessa picked up her shotgun and took a seat on the couch; her eyes trained on the door. All the females were partially shifted, using their heightened senses to listen and scent for trouble before it came to their door.

"I need to check on Ransom, but I don't want to call the healer's phone," Anna Claire fretted.

"He could still be in surgery," Ada reminded her.

"All we can do is wait," Tessa growled. They all knew they had to stay safe for their cubs, but it was killing Anna Claire not knowing what was going on outside their home.

Chapter 14

Gunnar's beast kept his nose to the ground as he tracked the two human males through their land. He was out for blood, and nothing was going to stop him from killing them. They'd crossed a line. That line gave him the right to end their lives.

At that point, he didn't care if it was done on his land or in the public square. Ransom was fighting for his life because of a bullet that had to have come too close to his heart. Shifters were great healers when injured, but they couldn't heal from a shot to the heart or head.

His mate was hiding, most likely in fear, in their quarters with the other females of his clan. The cubs were as safe as possible, but if there were more humans coming for them in two days, he didn't know if their home could hold off an attack.

Drake growled as they reached a road past the back of their property. The scent of the males was easy to track to the next spot of land. The sounds of the river reached his ears, but it didn't cover the sound of the two humans running through the brush.

They darted across the road and over a felled tree. Gunnar's beast pushed at his human mind, wanting to let his true nature lead, but he fought the animal. It was just Drake and Gunnar on the hunt. Luca and Rex had stayed back to dispose of the bodies, and they didn't know how much ammunition the two remaining humans had on them. If they weren't careful, Drake and Gunnar could end up like Ransom and no one would know where to find them.

His only hope was the sheriff and his damn visions. If that angel had seen something, he would surely come for them, wouldn't he? The Morgans never relied on anyone but themselves, but this was something where they might actually need assistance. Yet again, outside forces had disrupted their way of life, and Gunnar felt the anxiety of it all.

Drake and Gunnar ducked when a shotgun blasted from up ahead. They'd obviously been seen, but they were bears. It wasn't like they could hide all that well with their sizes. The only thing they had going for them was how quiet they could move and how vicious they were when threatened.

Gunnar dropped to his belly and forced the shift, ducking for cover when he came back to his human self. His brother's bear belly-crawled next to him, and they hid behind a clump of vines. Luckily, they were approaching summer and the forest was green and thick, giving them a chance to hide until they made a plan.

"They're a hundred yards upriver," Gunnar whispered so quietly only a shifter could hear his words. "I'm going around to head them off. Slow them down, but keep them on their toes. We don't want them to think we gave up on finding them just yet."

Drake's bear huffed his approval and narrowed his eyes in the humans' direction. They both knew they needed to eradicate the threat, because if they returned to the clan before Drake or Gunnar arrived, their mates and cubs could be at risk.

He took his human steps as carefully as he could. He might've been bigger in his beastly form, but being human, he could amble through the brush more carefully. Being an apex predator gave him that ability. His human feet were not covered, but the cuts and scrapes he was getting would heal within a minute or two while he made a huge arc around the humans.

He was aware it would take him a while to come out ahead of them, and he knew just the location to go. If he could make it toward the panther's lands, he could come close to their fence line and use that as a guide to the river. He would never cross their lands, because he'd heard they had that place on lockdown with cameras that covered every inch of their property. Gunnar was certain they'd see him if he got too close. He just hoped they were as friendly to him when he was outside their gates as they were when their healer was caring for his mate.

He ducked low and headed toward the southwest, keeping his body shielded behind large trees and growth on the forest floor. The sounds of the males eventually quieted as he got further away. A rabbit scurried under a rotting tree, and birds flew away as he moved. His human mind wandered to Anna Claire, but he had to stop daydreaming about his mate. Not paying attention could get him killed.

He saw the fence to the panther's land and skirted around the edges, noting the cameras placed at certain intervals. They would see him in all his glory, but he didn't have time to stop should one of them come to investigate. They could get the information from the sheriff.

Moving toward the river, he climbed over downed trees as quietly as he could. It took another ten minutes to come out ahead of them. With his partially shifted nose, he raised his head to the sky, relying on the wind to bring their scent in his direction. The bear inside him pushed for release, and Gunnar dropped to his knees to allow the animal to be free.

He waited for another minute before scanning the area close to the river. Their footsteps were making all kinds of noise as they approached. Gunnar laughed inside the bear's mind as he heard them talking amongst themselves.

"They're going to kill us, Pops," a male said, cursing when his leg got caught up in some vines. "Those bears just ripped the others to shreds."

"That's why we are getting the hell out of here,

Don," the other male replied.

"What if we see one?" Don, who was obviously the son, asked. They were getting closer, and Gunnar caught the scent of his brother who wasn't far behind them.

"Then we kill those abominations and take their bodies to the media," the father replied. "The money will be good."

"At least we don't have to split it with the others now," Don snickered as they fell quiet.

Gunnar waited up ahead, allowing the males to get closer. As it was, they were still too far away to ambush them. His heart froze in his chest as they came into view and the older male lifted a phone to his ear.

"Yeah?" he answered, looking toward the sky. "They killed the others. Yep. Their home is easily accessible from the woods if you want to go in and start picking them off tomorrow. I don't know. We shot one pretty close to his heart. I'm betting he's dead, but there were too many of them for us to grab the body. Sure, let me know when you arrive."

They were bringing reinforcements.

Fuck!

Gunnar didn't know how many were coming, but he knew they were going to need help. It was time to kill those two human males so he could return home and get the females to safety. The game had just changed, and despite all their precautions, the first of the month was going to be a deadly one.

Gaia sat in the middle of the small living quarters, closing her eyes and using her powers to build a storm of all storms for the upcoming day. It was nearing the first of June and the day the humans would go after all grizzly shifters. She knew of only a few clans, and she would do what she could to drive the humans away from any remote locations.

It wasn't just her clan she wanted to protect. There were others. The grizzlies were special to her, and since she'd stepped into the role of protection for the Morgan clan, she'd come to love them all…even the ones she'd never met.

"I need a list of places these hunters are going to strike tomorrow," she blurted. "Hurry! Write down the locations on a piece of paper."

She kept her eyes closed as the females scrambled to get the information she was needing. Why hadn't she thought of that sooner? She'd been so worried about her males that she didn't think to use the dark web's chat rooms to her advantage.

"Found the list," Ada called out.

Gaia never opened her eyes because she was too focused on the elements and how she was going to use them to her advantage. She hadn't caused this much of an earthly event in thousands of years. The last time was a little different. She'd had to wipe out the existence of some really bad shit.

This time, she was going to take out the trash…meaning the lowest scum of the human population. Anyone who thought it was okay to kill a species deserved what she had planned.

"Here," Ada announced as she approached, dropping a slip of paper in front of Gaia.

She didn't need to look at the paper to get the information. With her tiny hand, she crumpled the paper, letting her magic do the work for her.

"What are you doing?" Anna Claire asked.

"Making the humans wish they'd never messed with your species," Gaia smirked as she felt a cool wind blow across her skin.

All the cell phones in the room starting alarming with impending weather alerts. Gaia opened her eyes as the females gasped. The saucy smirk that raised the corner of her lip was pure evil, and she was going to enjoy every second of the destruction she'd planned.

"Oh, Gaia!" Tessa called out. "What have you done?"

Anna Claire watched as her mate's friend stood. Whatever Gaia had planned was going to be bad, and she worried for the others. "We have elders in their cabins. Do we need to move them to the main house?"

"No," Gaia said, shaking her head. "The clan will not see any damage."

"Only the humans?" Tessa balked. "It's not fair to the innocents."

"The innocents will not be harmed, I promise," Gaia replied, and Anna Claire believed her.

Anna Claire placed her hand on her belly, silently praying she wasn't bringing a cub into a world where it would be hunted simply for existing. The two other cubs were too precious and loved, and knowing what the humans had planned for them sent chills up her spine.

How could they hurt a child? A female?

She shook her head and remembered watching the human's newscasts. They had no love toward each other and acted more like animals than the actual shifters did. At least when her kind killed, it was for a reason.

The list was lengthy, and she didn't know how Gaia was going to manipulate the weather to stop the humans from killing the grizzlies.

The clap of thunder rattled the door to her quarters even though they were underground. Ada shivered and held Thane closer to her chest. Tessa glanced up from where she was feeding Aria and a look of fear passed between the three of them. Their world was changing, and they didn't know what they were going to do if more of the hunters came to their land.

Gaia picked up the list and nodded to herself, like she was proud of what she was about to do. Anna Claire trusted her, but it still worried her about the aftereffects of her destruction.

"There are seventeen states on this list," Anna Claire noted.

"And there are over a hundred hunters," Ada reminded her.

"We have to stay safe," Tessa said, glancing at Anna Claire's belly. She automatically covered her unborn child and nodded.

The females weren't as incapable as one would think. A mother bear was fiercely protective of their cubs, and even Anna Claire was feeling the rage at the thoughts of someone hurting her unborn child. She would do anything for the baby in her womb even though she hadn't met it yet.

The males were protectors, and they wanted the females to rely on them for their protection, and while Anna Claire understood their nature, she wanted to help them find and kill the hunters. Being with young stopped her from doing just that. She wasn't stupid, and she would never put her cub in harm's way.

The phone rang, interrupting their conversation.

Anna Claire pressed the button to answer when she saw the healer was calling. "Harold?"

"Anna Claire," he sighed into the phone. "Are you with your mate?"

"No," she gasped. "He's out searching for the hunters. Why? Is something wrong with Ransom? Oh, gods!"

"Is anyone with you?" he pressed, and she felt her heart plummet to her feet.

"Gaia and the females are," she said, feeling tears prick at her eyes. "We are in my quarters. What's wrong? Tell me!"

Her heart was beating so fast, she felt sick. There was a sadness to his voice, and she knew whatever he'd called to tell her was going to destroy her.

"I'm so sorry, Anna Claire," he began. She reached out for someone…anyone. Gaia grabbed her hand and jerked the phone from her hand, putting it on speakerphone. "I tried everything I could, but Ransom's injuries were just too much."

"What!" she screamed, dropping to her knees. "No!"

"Ransom passed away during surgery," Harold continued. "The sack around his heart tore when the bullet entered his body, nicking his heart. The injury was just too much for his bear to heal. Again, I am so sorry."

"No!" she screamed as the tears and cries ripped from her body.

She heard Gaia talking to the male, but Anna Claire was in too much distress to understand what they were talking about. Her cousin…one of the three males in her life who loved her…the male who'd done everything in his power to protect the young women of his clan was gone.

"Oh, gods…it hurts so bad," she screamed as the weight of the news crushed her.

Chapter 15

Lighting flashed across the sky as the clock wore down to the last hours for the month of May. Gunnar's eyes adjusted to the lack of light as he watched the human males make a camp to hide out for the night. They were scrambling to make a shelter from the incoming storm he knew had probably been made by Gaia. She knew something, and he needed to end these assholes' lives to get back to his land.

He'd shifted to his animal form once the humans started panicking because the day was ending and they were lost. Drake had backed off on his stalking two hours ago, giving the males the illusion that the shifters had given up. He and his brother didn't need to talk to each other to know exactly what they were going to do.

Hide.

Stalk.

Attack.

His beast focused on the humans, noting his brother's position south of the males. Drake's bear jutted his chin out to let Gunnar know he was watching them as well.

Gunnar's beast jerked his head to the side when he heard a faint sound far off in the distance. He had to suppress a deep warning growl as he lifted his nose to the sky, scenting the air. A faint, recognizable scent crossed his nose and he lowered his head as his enhanced vision saw a sleek, black panther crouched low to the ground as it stalked toward him.

As he scanned the area, he noticed two more panthers behind the first. As the first one stopped about fifty feet away, he dropped to his belly as he waited for the other two to join him. They shifted in unison and knelt as low as they could to stay hidden.

"What are you doing here?" Gunnar asked after he forced the shift. His voice was barely a whisper.

"We are here to help," Savage, one of the panthers, said.

"Help?" Gunnar frowned.

"We saw you on the cameras," Lucky, another panther, shrugged.

"Talon sent us," Booth, the third one, announced.

Gunnar wasn't shocked the local panther alpha had sent his men to help. They'd offered their assistance so many times over the past few years, and while the clan wasn't one for accepting any outside help, he was beginning to understand the need to have allies.

With Ransom being stitched up at their healer's office, he knew they would know everything that had happened over the past few weeks. The sheriff was loyal to them, and he must've told them everything.

"How's Ransom?" he whispered, knowing he

shouldn't be talking so much, but his mate's cousin had been in bad shape when the angel had whisked him away to Harold's place earlier.

"He's still in with the healer," Booth replied quickly, changing the subject as he narrowed his eyes at the two other panthers. "Tell us what's going on here."

"We have two humans who fled to the woods," he replied, turning to look over his shoulder. Off in the distance, he could see what was the beginning of a small campfire. It looked like the humans were settling in for the night instead of trying to find their way out.

He would worry about his mate's cousin after they took out those two males. He couldn't get distracted while on the hunt, which was one of the first rules his father had taught him after his first shift at the young age of five.

"We will do as you advise," Booth replied. "This is your right, and we will not stand in your way."

"But we sure will stand in theirs," Lucky, the younger panther, chuckled.

Gunnar nodded and accepted their help. The panthers returned to their shifted forms and lay quietly in wait. Drake waited in his bear form, never shifting or coming from his spot to check on the panthers. It was a huge step for his oldest brother to not be involved with the panthers. It gave Gunnar hope they could come to be friends.

His bear shook its head as he progressed forward, but Gunnar's human mind ached. Something wasn't right, and he could feel it. Pausing, he watched as the younger male typed away on a cell phone, dropping it into his pocket as the older male settled down on the hard ground.

"Get some sleep," he advised, closing his eyes. "It's already ten thirty, and we need to be up at dusk so we can get out of these damn woods."

"Just updating the others," the younger one said, yawning as he found his resting spot.

Gunnar held his beast back from attacking, preferring to wait until they were asleep. He figured ten minutes would suffice. They needed to get rid of those two so they could return home to help the others for when the day broke. June first was upon them, and it was time to protect their clan.

As the humans relaxed, Gunnar's bear looked back at the panthers who were lying in wait. They hadn't moved nor did they rise as he acknowledged them. They were going to let the Morgan brothers handle them.

Gunnar's bear moved slowly as he stalked his prey from one side. He watched Drake out of the corner of his eye as they descended on the makeshift camp. The small fire they'd built was fading out, turning into glowing red coals instead of a warming flame.

The path to the males was easy to navigate in

their larger forms, and Gunnar smirked inside his bear's mind. It was time for the predator to take out the enemy. When Drake joined him, their bears leaned over the sleeping hunters. There was no warning for them as the two grizzlies brought forth the punishment the human males so greatly deserved.

Gaia's heart ached for Gunnar's mate. Luca had arrived shortly after the phone call from the panther's healer. He and Anna Claire clung to each other over the horrible news. She'd lost a cousin and he'd lost his brother. Their small blood family had just taken another hit.

Tessa made everyone a meal as they waited for Gunnar and Drake to arrive. There was no way to get the message to them while they were out hunting. It was nearing midnight, and she hoped they were okay.

Rex was pacing by the front door, and his eyes were so golden, they glowed with the presence of his bear. He'd sent Ada and Thane to their quarters for safety once the clock struck midnight. He'd asked the other females to do the same, and Tessa had said she would do so after everyone was fed and cared for, meaning Anna Claire was calm enough to be left on her own.

Gaia closed her eyes and worked on the storms to ravage the areas she knew there were hunters coming for the grizzlies. She wasn't like the sheriff who'd been sent here to care specifically for the panthers. Gaia was here on a favor to the only friend she'd ever had.

There was only so much she could do. Manipulating the elements was a piece of cake for her, and she wished she had the magic to wipe them out with the fire and lightening from her hands, but she didn't. Unless she was in front of a threat, she couldn't risk it.

"Here they come," Rex announced, bringing everyone to their feet.

Anna Claire's cries intensified as Gunnar came in the door. He gasped and immediately rushed to his mate's side. "What happened?"

"Ransom…" she paused to take a breath as he cradled her against his chest. "He…he didn't make it."

"Fuck," Gunnar snarled, scooping her up into his arms and carrying her down the hallway to their quarters.

Luca covered his face with his hands and took a deep breath before standing up to meet Drake, who'd come to stand in front of him. "I want revenge."

"And you will have it," Drake vowed. "More are coming."

"Are you sure?" Gaia gasped, standing from her

seat on the couch.

"Positive," he replied, launching into the story of the two remaining hunters. He'd found the human's phone and had pulled up the message he'd sent over the private message app on the phone. "There are five more coming to the area today."

"When?" Rex asked.

"By dark," Drake replied and glanced at Gaia. "We cannot have destruction here."

"If I only knew where they were coming from…" she began, but froze when a flash of white light momentarily blinded her. "What is the sheriff doing here?"

Rex unbarred the door and immediately opened it, reaching a hand out for Garrett. The two men shook as they greeted each other.

"I've had a vision," he replied and waved everyone into the kitchen as Rex locked things up.

"We know," Drake said, tossing the sheriff a phone. "We found this on the human's phone."

Garrett's eyes were still as white as snow as he marched into the room. Gaia felt his energy, and she was taken aback for a second. When he looked up and caught her standing there, his eyes changed back to his human side…an odd hazel color that was more green than brown.

She'd never noticed them before now. It could've been the contrast between the two colors. The change from his angel white to his human color was staggering, and Gaia felt her heart flutter.

"That's not right," the sheriff said with a shake of his head. "I saw all of them in my vision."

"What did you see?" Rex ordered.

"There are more," Garrett panted, closing his eyes as tight as they would go. "A lot more."

"How many?" Gaia asked, moving closer to the sheriff when he shivered.

"Eight…possibly more," he cursed. "They're organizing and heading this way. They'll be here before dusk, and they aren't going to hide."

"They're coming to our doorstep?" Drake blared, his body swelling and pulsing with the need to shift.

"Right to the door," Garrett confirmed, jerking his head to the side so he could look directly at Drake. "I don't see them winning. Hell, I can't see anything past their arrival, but I have a feeling deep in my chest that it won't end well if you stay on your current path."

"What does that mean?" Gaia pressed, feeling the earth's energy swirling inside of her. She had to tone it down or she would cause the ground to shake beneath her feet again, and she didn't want to do that…not now. There would be time for that later.

"I can only see human involvement," Garrett began. "If a paranormal species intervenes, I am blind. My guess is you will have help, and if you don't, the clan could perish."

"What if we help ourselves?" Drake growled as

he tucked his chin so his long, dark hair could frame his face. "We *are* the paranormal."

"That's not how it works." Garrett sighed and ran his hand through his dark, brown hair. "My visions are given to me for a reason. I don't always know what they are, but the one thing that stays true is that when something human comes for the pride, I know the outcome. I can pinpoint what's going to happen, but if there are shifters involved, I lose sight."

"So, you're saying there are other species coming to help?" If he saw other species arriving, there was hope.

"Yes," Garrett answered and approached Drake. "I know how you feel, and I know you take care of your own…but, you need them. Drake…you need to talk to the pride."

Drake grabbed a chair and spun it around, dropping down into the seat. The wood creaked as he leaned over to rest his elbows on his knees, covering his face with his hands. "I've asked too much of them already."

"They'll come, and you know that." Garrett was right. Gaia had seen the things the pride had done.

"The Shaw pride has the manpower you'll need, Drake," Gaia added. She walked over and knelt in front of him and lowered her voice to a level only the shifter could hear. "Please, Drake. I cannot protect you from this. You need their help."

"It was never your place to protect us," he

reminded her, keeping his voice low. "My mother should've never asked that of you."

"But she did," Gaia replied. "I have loved you and your brothers since you were little."

"And we have loved you as if you were another mother to us," he replied and took her hands as they both stood. She felt tears prick at the back of her eyes as the large male took her into his arms. "We will be okay."

"You should talk to the alpha," she whispered as he released her.

Drake thought for a moment as the sheriff stood at the other end of the table, watching their interactions. She'd never told Garrett the entire story of why she was here, and her pride wouldn't let her. Gaia was a bit selfish and wanted someone to love and befriend because sitting around watching the world tear itself apart made her feel unwanted. It was fate she'd come upon Drake's mother and befriended her all those years ago. She would forever cherish the memories she'd gathered over the last thirty-eight years of being in her human form.

"Call Talon and tell him I'd like a meeting," Drake ordered. "And it needs to be done as soon as possible."

Anna Claire took a deep breath and wiped her eyes one last time. She'd cried so much, she didn't have any tears left to shed. "I can't believe he is gone."

"We will give him a warrior's pyre," Gunnar promised as he kissed the top of her head.

"That's what he deserves," she whispered and pushed away from her mate. The absence of his warmth caused a shiver to roll up her spine. Her hand automatically went to her stomach in a protective manner to cover her cub, and her mate noticed, covering her hand with his own.

"Everything is going to be okay," he promised. "I won't let anything happen to you or our cub."

"I'm more worried about you," she replied, feeling the ache in her eyes. She needed to cry again, but the tears wouldn't come. "What is going to happen now?"

"We will guard the clan tomorrow," he vowed. "No one will come for us. I'm going to ask that the elders come here before daybreak and stay inside where we can keep them safe."

"Please do," she gasped. "I cannot lose another person I care for."

"You've been through so much," he stated,

taking her back into his arms. "Let me hold you and our cub for just a little while longer. I need to have a talk with my brother to make a plan before the day breaks."

"Kiss me, Gunnar," she pleaded. Needing his warmth and touch was essential to her mental state. Getting lost in her mate right then probably wasn't the best course of action during this new war brewing outside their door, but she needed him with a passion she couldn't describe.

Chapter 16

Gunnar and Drake left the clan late that night after their mates were settled. The sheriff followed their truck to the panther's land for protection. Even though the lawman hadn't seen any visions of another attack that night, they weren't taking any chances.

"I think it's a good thing we are asking for their help," Gunnar announced. "They've offered their assistance without request of payback before, and they've always had our backs."

"They're putting themselves in harm's way for us," Drake reminded him. His brother's eyes were already golden as his beast was on edge. Gunnar had advised him to push his bear away before they arrived at the Shaw's land.

"We need allies," Gunnar stated.

"I know," Drake sighed and blinked a few times until his eyes returned to their natural brown color.

It was just after midnight when they pulled up to a security gate at the driveway but didn't have to talk to the male waiting in a small shack by the fence. He pressed a button to open the large iron gate and waved them through. The sheriff followed closely behind.

The drive up to the main house was covered with

large trees with their limbs hanging over the gravel road. Upon a clearing, the red brick home stood in the middle of a large meadow. To the left of the house, quite like their own, a road lead to several cabins. Each one was lit by a porch light and had their own unique design to the outside.

Gunnar didn't feel uneasy with the cats, but that didn't mean that his brother felt the same. A rumble came from his chest when he opened the door and the scent of the pride reached his nose.

"It's going to take some getting used to, Drake," Gunnar reminded him. "They are not our enemy."

"I know," his brother grunted. "Let's do this."

The front door opened and Talon Shaw, the pride's leader, stepped out along with Savage and Booth, two of the older Guardians. The Guardians were an elite group of males who had vowed to protect the alpha and the pride. They were lethal, and they'd proven that to the Morgan clan several times over the last few years.

"Drake," Talon greeted as they approached the home. "Gunnar."

"Talon," he and his brother said in unison. The males exchanged handshakes and walked inside, following the alpha to his office.

"I've been advised by Garrett as to what he's seen," Talon admitted. The sheriff stood against the far wall, keeping himself in a neutral position in the room. "We are fighting our own war, but I have extra men who have volunteered to assist you tomorrow."

"As much as it pains me to ask," Drake began, sitting up straighter in his seat. Gunnar knew it was hard for his brother to ask for help, but the oldest Morgan brother wasn't going to take any chances with his mate and cub. Gunnar felt the same way. "We need help. If what the sheriff says is true, we are looking at the possible destruction of our clan."

"That won't happen," Talon replied with a flash of his glowing amber eyes. The male's beast was as agitated as his own. Gunnar knew Talon Shaw was an amazing leader and had compassion. That wasn't seen very often. "I will send a team to you mid-afternoon. They have been advised to follow your instructions and to protect the mates and cubs at all costs."

"That's a lot to ask of you," Gunnar replied. His Guardians were willing to sacrifice themselves for a grizzly mate and cub. It was shocking to say the least.

"We may not be of the same species, but we are from the same gods," Talon reminded them. His eyes calmed as he stood from his seat. "It's best if we stick together when an enemy comes our way."

Drake stood, but he remained silent. Gunnar watched as his brother thought over the alpha's words. Talon was extending his friendship, but it was up to Drake and Gunnar to accept it.

"I agree with you," Drake finally replied, holding out his hand to seal the deal on a new friendship with the panthers.

"And I agree, as well," Gunnar stood and took the alpha's hand. "I appreciate all you have done for us over the past few years. My mate's health and safety are my top concern. Your healer should be held in highest regard for the things he has done for our clan."

"We are very lucky to have him," Talon nodded in agreement, but a wave of sadness crossed his features, reminding Gunnar of the recent news. "On behalf of the entire Shaw pride, I want to extend my condolences for the loss of your mate's blood family."

"Thank you," Gunnar said with a nod. He could still hear his mate's cries in his mind, and it caused a shiver to roll down his spine. "There was nothing that could be done for him, and we will plan his funeral pyre upon the end of this current war with the human hunters."

"Storm, Lucky, Diesel, and Axel are in the main living room," Talon advised. "If you need more males, let me know now."

"Those four will suffice," Drake agreed. "I can't thank you enough for your support in this."

"In these times, we must stick together," Talon preached. "I remember a time not long ago that we asked you to help us." That was true. Drake had helped keep an eye on one of the panther mates during a time where they'd been targeted.

"I think we have a deal," Drake replied, standing

a little taller. Gunnar saw the change in his brother the moment he connected hands with the alpha. Their alliance would be a good thing for the future of the clan and pride.

"My men will arrive at your place by four tomorrow evening," Talon replied. "They'll be coming in as panthers with no vehicles. I've instructed Storm to be your point of contact. He will shift and approach your home through the rear. Is that agreeable?"

"Yes," Drake nodded. "I have clothes they can borrow should they need to shift, or I can take them home with me now to keep at the main house."

"We will sort all of that out with them," Talon replied and nodded toward the sheriff, who opened the door so the four males could enter.

They got down to business, discussing a plan. Gunnar and Drake left with a duffle bag of clothes and a plan to keep their clan safe. He felt a lot more at ease knowing they had doubled their numbers with the panthers on their side.

The pain of losing Ransom would never fade. Anna Claire vowed to honor him for the rest of her life. She didn't know when they'd be able to give him his final sendoff back to the gods, but she prayed it would be soon.

"Anna Claire?" Luca called out as he knocked twice on the main door to her quarters.

She dropped the blanket she'd covered up with and hurried to the door, removing the bar and throwing the locks to get to her other cousin. Gods, they looked so much alike.

"Luca, what's going on?" she asked, seeing his eyes were golden and his canines extended.

"Drake and Gunnar are on their way back from the pride," he announced, and she felt her heart soar. They'd asked for help, and she was certain the Shaw pride wouldn't leave them alone in this war. "Talon Shaw will send some of his Guardians to help us, but the sheriff has seen things."

"What did he see in his vision?"

"There will be more coming," he admitted, taking her into his arms for a tight, brotherly hug. "The angel's vision stops after their arrival, but he feels some sense of doom. It all depends on the path we choose."

"I understand," she replied. The sheriff was different, but the gods gave him the visions to protect the panthers, and she assumed them as well. "What's the plan?"

"The plan is," he began, taking her by the shoulders so he could look deep into her eyes, "for you to stay put. There will be no gathering of the females, either. We want you spread out."

"What about the elders?" she reminded him.

"They've chosen to stay in their shelters," he replied. "I've given Alfred and Doug extra weapons and ammunition should it be needed."

"Where's Gunnar?" she asked, feeling on edge.

"He should be here soon," Luca promised, but gave her a little shake. "Do you understand me, cousin? We want the mates protected, and to do that, you have to stay inside this room until one of us comes for you."

"I get it," she huffed, feeling the weight of the impending doom on her shoulders.

Anna Claire walked back over to the couch and sat down after Luca had left. She didn't bar the door again because she knew Gunnar would be arriving at any moment.

It wasn't a few minutes before her mate walked through the door. It might've been only a few hours since she'd seen him, but it felt like days…weeks even. He stopped in the threshold and stared at her. His head tilted to the side in question, but he didn't speak.

Anna Claire, once again, climbed to her feet, but this time, she ran toward her mate and climbed into his arms. His deep inhale of her scent calmed her as much as hers did for him. Together they were stronger, happier. Knowing the hunters were coming soon scared her to death.

"I'm scared, Gunnar," she admitted against his neck. She placed a kiss to the mating mark she'd left on him the night they officially mated, and he shivered.

"I'm not," he replied, his voice deep and secure. "We have made friends with the Shaw pride, and the panthers are going to assist us when these hunters arrive. I promise you, it will all be over in a matter of minutes."

"Then we can live in peace?"

"Yes, honey," he promised, using the nickname he'd given her so long ago. "We will be safe, and you and our cub can live without fear."

The stood there in their living quarters for the longest time just holding onto each other. She knew she needed to rest for the sake of her unborn cub, but she just couldn't bring herself to close her eyes for fear of waking up to news of her mate being hurt by the hunters. The last thing she wanted to do was imagine him being in Ransom's shoes.

"When are they coming?"

"Tomorrow at dusk," he answered, which was technically that night. He was thankful the alpha had agreed to the meeting after midnight, because without the help of the pride, the clan would be destroyed in less than twenty-four hours. "We need to rest before then. I'm going to need to be alert."

"Let's sleep," she offered and took his hand. Gunnar was right. He needed to rest, and so did she, but Anna Claire knew she wasn't going to get any sleep.

No sooner than his head hit the pillow, Gunnar was fast asleep. Anna Claire waited another ten minutes before sliding quietly out of the bed, then the room. Once the door was closed, she looked at the clock and groaned that it was only a couple of hours before sunrise. Her worry wouldn't let her sleep.

The phone they'd been using was hidden in the upper cabinet over the fridge. Anna Claire quietly pulled a chair from the small dining table over and climbed up to reach for the phone. She returned the chair and powered up the phone.

Wanting to know what was going on, she found the message boards and got to work, scanning all of the comments in a post that had been made at midnight.

D-Day – Post photos and results with locations here.

She paused before she clicked on the comments. There would be things in there she probably didn't want to see. The hunters were on a mission to kill the werebears, and she knew they'd be posting their images like a chartered trophy hunt. Could she really look at the photos?

Shaking her head, Anna Claire told herself that being informed was more important, because not having information could be deadly. She hoped she could find out where the new batch of hunters coming for them were staying or any clues as to when exactly they'd arrive. The sheriff said dusk, but she wanted to be sure.

Covering her mouth to hold in a cry of shock, she scanned the first image. A family of grizzlies lay in a row. A large male bear was lifeless next to a woman and two teenage cubs. All of them had been shot.

Tears poured out of her eyes as she read the location.

Price, Utah – Family of 4

The next comment stopped her. There wasn't an image. The hunter had posted there had been a tornado come through and destroyed their trucks. The location pinned them outside of Tulsa, Oklahoma.

The next comment was more of the same. Terrible destruction due to the weather in Rolla, Missouri; Lincoln, Illinois; Janesville, Wisconsin…and the list continued. Storm after storm hit every one of them. So much so, the human hunters started arguing about the reasoning behind it. Some said it was a coincidence, others said it was the hand of God.

Anna Claire knew it was the work of Gaia.

They were running. Gaia's plan of destruction was working.

With her tears drying, she scanned more and more posts of wind, tornados, hail, and severe thunderstorms preventing the hunters from achieving what they'd set out to do. One post stood out from the rest.

We are set to attack in northern Mississippi. The others have gone radio silent, and I am uneasy about the information we may find. We will wait out the day and go in at dusk.

She knew the ones who'd come before were dead. Gunnar and his brothers had taken out the human males before they could kill another member of her clan. She pressed her hand to her chest to still the panic at the loss of her cousin. The last thing she needed to do was to mourn him during this next round of attacks coming for them.

With that piece of information, Anna Claire returned the phone to its hiding spot, tiptoeing to the bedroom and sliding beneath the covers before her mate knew she was ever gone.

Chapter 17

Gunnar awoke to his alarm. He and Anna Claire had been up into the early morning hours, and he wanted to make sure he made the scheduled meeting with the panthers at four. They'd be in place soon, and then they would wait for the human males to arrive.

Gaia was already at the counter, making a cup of coffee when he left his sleeping mate to head into the main house. She'd stayed overnight, taking the couch despite the male's insistence she have a bed.

"Morning, Gunnar," she began after abandoning her cup and coming over greet him. She reached down and took his hands into hers and sighed heavily. "Know that if something bad happens tonight, I will extend my promise to watch over your family."

"I don't know why you stayed," he replied, relaxing a little as she dropped her hold and looked at the floor. "You promised our mother you would watch over us, but you didn't have to."

"I wanted to," she blurted, looking up at the ceiling for a second before leveling her emerald green eyes on him. "A vow is a vow, and integrity is important to me."

"Integrity is important, but staying here in human form is dangerous," he reminded her. "You are needed everywhere. Remember that."

"I'm trying," she sighed and returned to the counter for her cup. "Doesn't change anything. I'm staying here for a long time. I have no desire to return to the earth."

"Why?" he inquired, honestly curious as to why she wanted to stay here to watch over the planet and not return to the place where she ruled nature.

"It gets lonely there," she admitted. "I've found a family, finally. Something called to me all those years ago, telling me to come here. After I met your mother, I thought that was the reasoning behind it, but I'm not so sure now."

"Whatever it is, I'm glad you're here," he said with a smile. "Plus, there's no need to vow protection for the mates and cubs. We are going to beat this."

They were interrupted when Drake and Rex entered from their quarters. His two brothers hit the coffee pot for their cup and took a seat at the table. Luca came in not long after, and it was obvious from the look on his face, the male hadn't slept well the night before.

"Are you going to be able to do this?" Drake asked Luca the moment he sat down.

"I'm fine," he mumbled and hung his head. "I have to avenge him. Those hunters need to be taken out tonight."

"They do," Drake rumbled. "I don't want anyone else getting hurt, and if you are going to have a hard time focusing on the fight tonight because you are mourning, I don't want you…"

"I told you I was fucking fine!" Luca snarled and pushed back from the table, dumping the contents of his cup in the sink, and left out the back door before Drake, or anyone else for that matter, could stop him.

Drake and Rex's eyes shifted toward the door, but Gunnar held up his hand to get their attention. "He's hurting, and he has every right to do so. As far as tonight, I'm not worried about him. He will be a fierce fighter when the hunters arrive."

"We have a few hours before the panthers arrive." Rex stood and stretched. "Let's get everyone up and inside for a meeting over lunch."

Gunnar agreed with a nod and found his place in the kitchen. Cooking would take his mind off the events that were coming. Even if it was a little bit of peace, he would accept it and have a clan meal ready for them when everyone gathered.

It was a little later when tiny, warm hands wrapped around his waist as he stirred a pot of stew at the stove. Her scent and touch soothed him even more. Turning around, he closed his eyes and took her lips. "Good morning, honey."

"Morning," she mumbled and rested her head on his chest. "That smells amazing."

"It'll be ready in twenty minutes." The stew was

forgotten as he took her over to the large table. From a glance out the window, he noticed Drake and Rex were on their way with the elders. Anna Claire noticed them too, and she smiled widely. "I know why they're here, but I don't care. I've missed them so much."

"Take the next few hours to catch up before we have to send them home to shelter," he replied, knowing how much she loved the two couples from her old clan.

His mate clung to Peggy and Martha once they arrived. The two elder males sat at the kitchen table, watching protectively over their mates. Both of the males' weathered faces brightened when they saw the females they'd mated so many years ago. Gunnar joined them, then rested his head in his hands for a few seconds before sighing and clearing his throat. "We have no idea what will happen tonight."

"We are willing to fight alongside you," Alfred stated, leaning forward in his chair. The male was in his seventies, and while they could use the help, he needed them to stay hidden.

"I appreciate your offer, but I would prefer you stay with your mates," Gunnar replied, casting a glance at Anna Claire. The thought of someone hurting her brought an unexplainable rage to his mind. "The females need to be protected, and you are the best ones to care for your own mates. The panthers are coming, and we have come up with a plan for Tessa, Ada, and Anna Claire."

"And what is that?" Doug asked.

"They will be locked in their quarters. We don't want them together. It's too dangerous to keep the mates in one spot," he answered.

The elder males nodded and resumed drinking their coffee as the females chatted in the front living room. The clock on the wall moved slower than it should, and Gunnar was feeling the adrenaline start to pulse through his veins with each passing minute.

Once everyone was fed, he spent time putting away the food and washing the dishes. Anna Claire asked if he needed help, but he sent her off to visit more with the females. He could see the fear in her eyes as she tried to put on a brave front for the females.

Drake, Rex, and Luca arrived a little later, shaking the elder males' hands in greeting. As Gunnar looked around the room, he realized just how much his new family had blended so well. The elders had done as they said and helped out over the last year to make their clan even better. The crops they'd planted were growing, and in the fall, they'd harvest what would probably be their best yield in years.

Their crops wouldn't mean a thing if the hunters succeeded in killing them. Gunnar was making it his personal goal to ensure everyone in his clan was safe from that moment forth.

Gaia returned to the pride after going to secure her home. The hunters were coming, and they hadn't heard from the sheriff in hours. She'd hoped he was there by the time she arrived, but he wasn't.

"Where are the panthers?" Gaia asked as she entered through the back door. Gunnar had her park her car behind the barn and Luca walked her toward the house in case any of them were already in place.

"They'll be here soon," Drake grunted. "We should get in place."

"I'm going with you," she blurted, but froze when the males turned to glare at her. She called upon the elements and a clap of thunder rumbled the windows. "I have to be outside."

"Absolutely not," Drake snarled with a slash of his hand. "It's too dangerous."

"I've stopped ninety percent of the attacks, and this is the most important one," she yelled. They knew how much they meant to her, and if she couldn't control the weather, they might perish. "You cannot stop me."

"Damn it, Gaia," Rex bellowed. "We can't protect you while we are stopping them."

She dug deeper into her soul and thickened the clouds around the land. Lightning cracked close and everyone jerked where they stood. Her eyes swirled and clouded over as she pulled at the elements to get them ready for the moment the humans arrived.

"Gaia!" a voice blared next to her ear. When she shook herself from the fog, Garrett was there holding onto the tops of her arms. "Are you okay?"

"I'm fine, why?"

"You almost collapsed," he replied. "What's going on with you?"

Once she got her bearings and glanced around the room, she realized her body was at the wrong angle. The ceiling was in front of her, and Garrett must've taken her to the couch in the living room.

"What happened?" Confusion set in, and she tried to remember what her humanly body was doing while she was far away, building a storm to protect the clan.

"That's what I want to know," Drake interrupted, kneeling in front of her.

When she sat up, a wave of nausea came over her. She pressed her hand to her stomach and took a few deep breaths. "I was building a storm."

Her words were understood, but the Morgan brothers tensed. Gunnar frowned at her and came to his brother's side, but he didn't kneel. "You've done too much over the past twelve hours."

"I have to get into place," she said, pushing the males away. "It's almost time."

"There is no way you are going to be outside,"

Garrett ordered.

"You don't have the right to tell me what I can or cannot do," she reminded him.

"Wanna bet?" he pushed, reaching behind him to remove a set of handcuffs from his utility belt.

"You wouldn't!" Gaia narrowed her eyes.

"If you don't stay in the house with the other females, I will," he replied, his eyes flashing white.

She felt that flutter in her heart, and she took a step back, thankful she didn't lose her balance. Ignoring him, she walked around the males and made her way into the kitchen where their mates were waiting. The elders must've left when she went into her trance.

A knock on the back door stopped her from explaining anything to the females. Drake marched over and pulled the door open wide. A shirtless male stood there with three others at his back.

"Booth," Drake greeted.

"Are you ready to do this?" Booth asked, looking over his shoulder. "Looks like there's a storm coming. It's going to be a rough night."

Anna Claire watched as the males took seats around the living room while Drake and Gunnar stood. They worked with the sheriff, confident their plan on stopping the hunters was solid.

While Garrett went over his vision, she noticed how Gaia's eyes tracked his every move. The female didn't put off any type of mating scent, so Anna Claire wondered what was going on.

"Are you going outside with them?" Tessa asked, interrupting Gaia's staring.

"You better believe your ass I am," she snarled. "I have to control the weather to keep the hunters from succeeding."

"I saw the destruction of the other hunters around the world," Anna Claire whispered. The other females gathered around her as she told them of what she'd read when she looked on the message boards earlier in the morning.

"They're running?" Gaia smirked.

"A lot of them thought it was odd, and a sign to back away," Anna Claire advised.

The look of pride crossed Mother Nature's face as she folded her arms across her chest. She looked very proud of her work, but even Anna Claire wouldn't show the males she was right in her actions. If they knew the females were still checking up on the hunters, it would cause too much of a headache when they blew their lids, so to speak.

"Good," Gaia smirked. "Now, if you'll excuse me, I am going to slip out the back door while they're occupied." She tossed a wink over her shoulder as she left.

"We aren't going to tell them?" Ada fretted.

"Not at all," Anna Claire replied. "She knows what she's doing."

"I hope so." Ada sighed. "It's almost time."

Gunnar entered the kitchen and came over to take Anna Claire by the hand. "It's time to go to our quarters."

She stepped away to hug the other females. Rex and Drake took Ada and Tessa, letting the panthers know they would be back shortly. The sheriff leaned against the kitchen counter and waited for everyone to get into place.

"I want you to stay in our room until I, or my brothers, come for you," Gunnar began as they walked down the hallway to their quarters.

"Please, be careful," she said as he closed the door. Gunnar hummed and pulled her close. The mating touch singed across her skin as he captured her lips.

"I will be back in your arms before the clock strikes midnight," he vowed and deepened the kiss.

Anna Claire closed her eyes and absorbed his touch. She was falling in love with him more and more every day. He was a large, scary male, but to her, he was a gentle giant. In all of her daydreams, she never imagined her mate being more perfect for her.

He pushed back and placed his large hand on her

small baby bump. He closed his eyes and said a silent prayer before turning away and walking out the door.

Chapter 18

"Where's Gaia?" Drake asked as soon as he returned to the living room.

The males narrowed their eyes on the back door, but it was Garrett who cursed the loudest. "You get into place. Let me worry about finding Gaia."

"She isn't like us," Gunnar reminded him. "If she takes a bullet, it could be the end of life for everyone."

"I know," Garrett groaned as he left the house.

Gunnar trusted the male with Gaia, but he knew Garrett was up to his eyeballs with her. She'd been on her own for eons and stopping her from doing something to help was going to be a fight.

The panthers shed their clothes, dropping them into the bag Drake had brought from their homes. After their shift, Rex, Drake, and Gunnar grabbed their weapons and headed toward the front of the house. Out on the porch, they stood their ground. They'd never hidden from an enemy before, and they weren't going to start now. Those hunters would have to go through them to get to the mates.

A bolt of lightning flashed across the sky as the last rays of light disappeared over the horizon. The scent of rain tickled Gunnar's nose, but he ignored the storm to search for the humans. It was nearing the time Garrett said his visions predicted. After that, they were on their own.

Drake's deep throated growl alerted them to the presence of humans. At the road, a group of men approached their lands. They were on foot, and every one of them were carrying rifles. With his enhanced vision, Gunnar saw each and every one of them as they marched forward.

Black panthers slinked up from the woods on each side of their home. The humans didn't see them, and that was the plan. Those cats blended in well with the night. Rex shifted to his right as he palmed his shotgun. Gunnar cracked his neck from side to side, preparing for the fight.

"Get off our land," Drake bellowed. They'd planned everything down to the words they would say to the humans. "I won't tell you again."

"You are an abomination!" one yelled, raising his gun. He was ahead of the group by fifteen feet. Before he could fire off a shot, a panther pounced at the male's gun, ripping it from his grasp. From the sound of the male's screams, the cat must've taken a chunk out of his arm.

"We can do this all night," Drake called out.

As the first human dropped to his knees and cradled his mangled arm to his chest, another one came forward, raising his gun. Again, a panther swiped the weapon away as a gust of wind came from behind the house, blowing right into the humans' faces. Their steps faltered as leaves swirled around their legs.

"I would advise you to go back from where you came," Drake continued. "Take a message back to the hacker that we are stronger and will fight back."

As planned, Drake, Rex, and Gunnar descended from the porch. Gunnar's bear was sitting right below his skin, preparing for a fight to the death. They wanted those males' blood. He knew the sheriff would intervene should the humans get the upper hand, but like in their ancient times, shifter law was in force.

The humans brought the fight to their lands, but the shifters would win. When it came to the protection of their mates and land, any species of shifter would kill to keep their families safe. Gunnar's chest ached at the thought of someone harming his mate and unborn cub.

"We aren't going anywhere until we have your pelts on our walls." The oldest one of the group, probably in his mid-forties, reached at his side, abandoning his rifle to draw a pistol from a holster at his hip, but…again, the panthers were there to swipe the weapon away.

"Wrong answer," Gunnar mumbled. He was primed and ready for a fight. He wasn't going to shift. The plan was to keep themselves human unless it was necessary. The panthers were backing them up, and the Morgan bears shouldn't need their animals to win this fight.

Luca was out back, keeping an eye on the elders' cabins. Although the sheriff hadn't seen the humans coming from the woods, they wanted them protected. He didn't know where Garrett had run off to, but he sure hoped the angel was on alert.

"Turn around and leave," Rex warned.

Another human male moved slightly from behind the crowd. Gunnar didn't miss his step, and he knew the dark-haired male was going to break away from the crowd to try and fire his weapon.

A flash of lightning bathed the area in enough light for the humans to see the four panthers at the males' sides. Two of the men took steps back, but the one who'd moved earlier advanced another step.

Gunnar's eyes were on him. Drake jutted his chin out slightly, directing Gunnar in that direction. The wind howled as he stalked the male. The human tucked his chin and smirked as Gunnar's bear pushed at his human skin. The golden color to his eyes proved the shift was close, but he held the bear back. He needed to end this in his human form.

"Last chance," the human yelled. The males around him surged and began to walk toward the house. With each step, they moved faster, but they weren't fast enough to catch any of the shifters.

"Bring it," Gunnar snarled and took off at a dead run as rain poured down across their lands. Wind swished and swirled. A clap and rumble of thunder was the only warning they had before the panthers jumped into action, taking down some of the humans.

Drake engaged one of them, taking him to the ground. Rex did the same to the other, but Gunnar had the cocky son of a bitch who'd tried to break away from the crowd.

The male darted behind a tree, bringing his gun up and firing off a shot at him.

He missed, and didn't that just piss off the beast inside him even more?

Gunnar roared as he approached the tree at inhuman speed. His canines were thick in his mouth as he grabbed the male, spinning him around. He was fully prepared to rip the male's throat out when he saw something move on the porch.

"Noooo!" he yelled as a human male entered their home. With a twist of his hands, he snapped the male's neck and dropped him to the ground.

Gunnar ran, using his second nature abilities to get him to the house. Fear pushed him harder. He focused on the house, not caring for the sounds around him. He didn't care if there was one or a hundred humans in his yard. The fact that one had gotten past them to enter sent him into a feral rage.

"Where is he?" Gunnar snarled through his partially shifted face. His ears ached with the pressure of the storm brewing outside. His clothes were soaking wet, but he didn't care. Killing that male for coming so close to the mates and cubs was at the forefront of his mind.

As the front door closed silently behind him, Gunnar heard the wind howling out on the lawn. He knew Gaia was somewhere hiding out so she could control the elements and scare away the humans. Maybe they'd consider it witchcraft and run away with their tails tucked between their legs.

The human made a noise in the kitchen, and his breathing became rapid. Gunnar moved quietly across the living room, coming to the threshold of the kitchen. The male slipped down the hallway toward Anna Claire, and Gunnar felt his heart drop.

Gunnar charged the human, running at full speed. The male turned, his eyes widening at the sight, but it only took half a second for the man to draw a pistol from his side and fire, hitting Gunnar in the middle of his chest.

A mighty roar tore from his throat as his bear tried to explode from his body, but the injury was just too much. The pain bloomed and blood splattered on the hallway walls as he slumped to the floor. The last thing he heard was the human scream and the sound of a grizzly's roar.

Anna Claire heard someone coming toward the door. She breathed a sigh of relief, hoping it was Gunnar arriving to tell her it was all over. The massive storm raging outside could still be heard in their underground quarters. Even though the room was underground, the hallways were not.

A thump against the door was odd, but she walked over anyway, waiting for the knock she'd been desperately awaiting. When the noise stopped, she shifted her ears and heard panicked breathing on the other side.

Lifting the bar off the door, she touched the deadbolt, but didn't throw the lock. Something wasn't right. If Gunnar had been outside, he would've called out to her already. Wouldn't he?

A roar sounded, then the explosion of a gun followed right behind it. She heard a body hit the floor, and her bear roared in her head to open the door. She didn't want to accept what she'd heard, but the animal inside her pushed at her human skin again.

Despite her better judgement, she opened the door, and she screamed when she saw her mate on the ground with a gunshot wound to his chest.

In a fraction of a second, her animal ripped from her skin, zoning in on the human male who stood over her mate's body. Anna Claire's human side cried out in horror again as Gunnar reached for her but he was too weak. The bear launched herself at the human, latching on to his throat and ripping it from his body.

The moment the human's body fell to the ground, she shifted and reached for her male. "Gunnar! Gunnar!"

He was still breathing, but it was labored. "Get…help. Call…Garrett."

She ran back into their room and grabbed the phone, throwing on some clothes as she waited for the male to answer. When it went to voicemail, she called the only other person she knew who could help.

"Anna Claire," the pride's healer asked the moment he picked up the phone. "Is everything okay over there?"

"No, Gunnar's been shot in his chest," she cried. "Please help us!"

"Where is everyone else?" he asked, but Anna Claire could hear him shuffling around in the background.

"I don't know," she cried, taking her old torn clothes and pressing them to the wound on her mate's chest.

"I'm coming," he replied, reminding her to keep him awake.

She dropped the phone and prayed someone would come help her. The last thing she wanted to do was call for the other females, because it was obvious one of the humans had gotten into their home.

"Gunnar, please stay awake," she begged as she pressed her lips to his own.

"Get inside," he ordered, but his deep voice was weak. "Lock…door."

"No, I'm not leaving you until someone comes," she growled. "I need you to shift. You have to shift, Gunnar."

"Trying…" he said before closing his eyes.

Anna Claire's face was wet with tears, but she was determined to do as the healer said. Shaking his arm didn't work. So, she pinched him as hard as she could. When his eyes popped open, they were the golden hue of his beast. She needed to get him to shift.

"Damn, Gunnar!" she roared. "Don't you leave me. Don't you leave *us*! We need you." She kept talking to him until she saw his canines thicken in his mouth. His bear was wanting out, but it was just too weak to force the shift.

"Do it, Gunnar!" she pressed. "Let your beast take over."

She shook him again, rousing him from his sleep. The blood still oozed from the wound as she lifted the cloth to take a look. Her hands were covered in his blood, and she prayed it would be enough.

"Don't leave me like Ransom, please…please," she cried and shook him again, causing him to open his eyes. "Shift, Gunnar."

The pain of loss was still fresh in her mind, and if she lost the love of her life, she wouldn't be able to go on. "I love you, Gunnar. Please don't leave me."

His head rolled to the side at her words, and a soft smile pulled at the corner of his lips. His face was slowly reforming, and she leaned over when he whispered something.

"I…love…with…everything…I…am."

She jerked back when his body shimmered, hugging the wall to give the thousand-pound grizzly enough room. Anna Claire breathed a sigh of relief when the bear rested his head in her lap.

The human male's body wasn't far away, but she noticed the gun beside his body. Scrambling as gently as possible, she reached for the gun and returned to her original position. Gunnar's bear closed its eyes as though it was satisfied she was protected so he could begin the healing process.

Anna Claire rested her back against the doorframe and waited for someone to arrive. She held the gun at the ready in case another hunter came looking for his friend. She wasn't afraid of them, but she was scared she was about to lose the mate of her life.

As she stroked the grizzly's head, Anna Claire prayed for a miracle. It was only a second later that the tornado sirens blared and all hell broke loose.

Chapter 19

Luca heard the gunshot, and only seconds later, the sound of Anna Claire's beast sent him running for the house. He would know her roar over anyone else's. They'd been through so much together, and he was tuned into her every move.

The wind, rain, and hail from Gaia's weather storm pelted his body as tornado sirens went off in the distance. The fighting in the front yard was still going on. The panthers and Morgan brothers were taking out the humans one by one, and a few of them were on the run.

As he entered the back door, he turned for their hallway and stopped in his tracks the moment he saw the bloodbath by their bedroom door. He held up his hands as he approached, because Anna Claire was pointing a pistol at his chest.

"Anna Claire, put down the gun," he ordered, glancing down at her mate who was in his animal form. There was blood everywhere; the floor, the walls, the door. A few feet away was the corpse of a human male with his throat ripped out. "Let me help Gunnar."

At the mention of her mate's name, she jerked out of the shock she was in and dropped the gun.

Fresh tears escaped her eyes as she pleaded with him. "Help me, Luca. I can't save him."

Luca dropped to his knees and placed his hand on the bear's fur. Gunnar was still breathing, but his bear was unconscious. He swallowed a lump in his throat at the resemblance between Gunnar and Ransom.

"Wake up!" he snarled at the bear, shaking him vigorously. When Gunnar's bear started to move, Luca backed away. "Shift, Gunnar. You need to heal."

The bear rumbled, opening his eyes. Anna Claire put her hands on either side of the bear's snout and begged, "Please, Gunnar. Shift now."

She let go when his body shimmered. Luca noted how it took longer for the male to regain his human form.

"The healer is on his way, but I don't know if he will be able to get to the house," Anna Claire said as she took Gunnar's head into her lap. "Please, go find him."

Luca climbed to his feet and hurried to the front of the house just as the rain and hail came to a screeching halt. Out on the one-acre lawn, bodies dotted the landscape. Rex and Drake were leaned over at the waist, panting heavily. The four panthers were pacing and snarling at the dead.

Sheriff Lynch stood protectively next to Gaia as they surveyed the damage. During the storm, not one branch fell from any tree…not one blade of grass was out of place. She'd controlled the storm, directing it at the humans. He didn't know how she had done it, but he was glad she did.

Drake jerked his head around and called out for Gunnar as soon as he realized the male wasn't in their presence.

"He's been shot in the house!" Luca yelled. "The healer is on his way."

A truck pulled in as they all took off toward the house. The panthers shifted and gathered their clothes, meeting their healer as he came to a stop. The older male hurried up the stairs to the porch and walked inside without saying a word. The look of worry on his face disappeared as soon as he crossed the threshold.

"I'll clean this up," Garrett advised. "You go in and check on Gunnar."

Gaia touched his arm as he passed, giving him a little strength. It was odd to have the female touch him and it not make him want to shy away. She wasn't like them, and he didn't know if she could even take a mate. She was an earthly being, and not made by the gods. Hell, she was a goddess, wasn't she?

Luca pulled his long, black hair back and used the tie on his wrist to keep it out of his face before walking inside to see if he was needed with Gunnar. If he wasn't, he would go check on the elders and let them know if was safe to come outside. He didn't need to worry about the mates anymore since the males were close.

It was just him, and going back to that lonely cabin made his heart ache.

Ransom, I fucking miss you.

Gunnar came awake with a jerk. His vision blurred as he tried to roll over to his side. The ground was a lot softer than it was the last time he was awake. *Odd.*

"Gunnar?" Anna Claire's sweet voice reached his ears as he struggled to see. Blinking several times, he felt like a weight was on top of his chest, but it didn't matter. He could scent his mate and cub, and that lulled him back into a deep sleep.

"Gunnar, please wake up," her voice called out again.

This time when he blinked, he could make out the outline of her perfect face. The longer he stared, the clearer she became. "Don't cry, honey."

"He's awake," she called out over her shoulder, and he wondered why she was telling anyone that. Wasn't he in his bed? "Gunnar, can you hear me?"

"Yes," he replied, feeling his beast begin to stir. The overwhelming need to shift caused him to reach for his shirt, but he wasn't wearing one. Anna Claire pulled his hand away from his chest, but not before feeling something like tape and gauze over his midsection.

"You were shot," she sniffled. "The bullet was in there, and the pride's healer had to go in and get it out."

"Fuck," he groaned. "My mate...are you...my cub...are you okay?"

"We are fine," she replied and pulled his hand over to press to her stomach. She was just starting to show with their cub, and he wanted nothing more than to press his lips to her skin.

"Gunnar," the healer said as he entered the room. By now, Gunnar's eyes had cleared, and he was in one of the rooms at the pride. "It's imperative you shift now that you're awake. The healing needs to begin."

"Yeah, okay," he said in a gravelly voice. Clearing his throat, he rolled to his side, dropping his feet to the floor. The healer and his mate tried to help him up, but he waved off their help. "Can I borrow your yard?"

"Of course," the healer said, smiling as he moved out of the way.

Anna Claire walked behind him as he shuffled through the door. Drake, Rex, and Luca stood from their posts outside the door. He waved them off as well and continued down the hallway leading to the back door of the healer's home.

He glanced back at the living room and saw where the four panthers who'd helped them stood alongside his brothers. He'd secretly hoped they would come to an agreement to become allies, and by the relaxed state of his oldest brother, he was certain there'd been friendships and bonds made over that fight.

"If I fall, you won't be able to catch me," he grunted to his mate.

"Well, I will try," she replied. Gunnar heard the little catch in her voice, and he stopped at the door to turn around so he could take her into his arms. "I love you, honey. Stay close while I shift. I need you there."

"I'm not going anywhere, Gunnar," she replied and kissed him with a feverish need.

After an hour of shifting, he was able to breathe easier. The wound had all but healed. A tiny, pink line was the only reminder of the hell they'd been through over the last few weeks. As he stood, Anna Claire was there with his clothes, and her arms wrapped around his body the moment he was covered.

He couldn't ask for anything else. He'd been granted his mate, and she would give him a cub over the winter. As he took her chin with his thumb and forefinger, he closed his eyes and inhaled the scent of his pregnant mate. "Let's go home."

That night, Anna Claire prepared for the ancient ritual to send her cousin to the afterlife. It should've been done the night he passed, but the panther's healer had kept his body preserved until the fight with the humans was over.

Luca and Anna Claire held each other tight before walking into the barn to prepare Ransom's body for the funeral pyre. It was tradition that the family wrapped the male in the gauzy, white cloth.

The males had built the pyre earlier in the day. It should've been Anna Claire out there helping, but with her pregnancy, she agreed not to lift the heavy pieces of wood. Instead, with the help of the other females, they found enough wildflowers to decorate the wooden structure for her cousin.

"Are you going to be able to do this?" Luca asked as they stopped in front of Ransom's body. He was laying there in such a peaceful state, she was afraid to speak. The healer had cleaned him up and someone had dressed him in his usual clothes. Other than the paleness to his features, you wouldn't have known he'd died.

"It's my honor as his cousin to see him into the next life," she said, proud of herself for not breaking down. The tears pricked at her eyes, but she didn't let them fall.

Luca picked up two rolls of gauze and handed her one. Together, they started at his face and began the ritual. Anna Claire leaned over and placed a kiss to his forehead and whispered, "I owe you my life more than I should."

Luca rested his hand on one side of the male's face and leaned down to whisper his final words to his blood brother. "Without you, I am nothing. You were my hero, and I hope I was yours."

They were silent as they worked, and no one bothered them until they were done. It was the blood family's right to prepare him, and even though Gunnar was her mate, he wasn't allowed inside. She wished he'd been there, but the Morgans stuck to traditions, and she loved her new clan because of it.

The last time she'd done this was for her mother. A lone tear leaked out of her eye as she thought of Ransom reuniting with her. She prayed he passed on the message of her happiness when he got to the afterlife.

With Ransom's body covered, Luca and Anna Claire bowed to the body and backed out of the barn. They would light the pyre at dusk and send Ransom home.

When the barn door opened, Gunnar was there to take her hand. When she touched him, the mating connection was strong enough to calm her shaking hands. He took her over to the wooden pile they'd built and waited for the sun to drop.

Anna Claire would not be a part of the death march to bring Ransom's body to the pyre. The males would bring him and place him upon the structure that looked more like a very tall bed. Once in place, Luca would bring her to the pyre and they would both light the fuel-soaked logs at the base.

"Are you ready to do this?" Gunnar whispered to her as he held her tight. The sun was dropping below the horizon faster than she wanted it to.

"No, but it must be done," she replied.

The males broke away. Tessa and Ada came to her side to place their hand on her forearms for strength. She didn't speak to them as she watched the last rays of light disappear from the sky.

Tessa broke away to light the two torches beside the pyre. Anna Claire felt a heaviness in her chest as she heard the march of the males' footsteps. The closer they got, the more she wanted to break down and cry. She wanted to scream at the unfairness of it all, but she wouldn't make that scene. She would save her anger at her cousin's death until she was alone with her mate.

Epilogue
Late January

Gunnar held his son in his arms for the longest time while Anna Claire slept. Ransom Chase Morgan, or RC as they'd begun to call him, was only a month old, but he'd already captured everyone's heart. His mate had named her first cub after the cousin she'd loved so dearly.

In the past two years, they'd been through so much, and bringing this new life into the world had made Gunnar feel complete. The birthing experience had been scary, as the males of the clan always delivered their own cubs. His father had taught them everything they needed to know as soon as they'd come of age to mate. The things he didn't know or had questions about over the course of her labor, his brothers had given him guidance.

With the next several weeks of hibernation, he would take turns with their cub as his mate slept. As it was, he let her sleep as much as she needed because of the stress on her body from bringing him into the world.

RC was born on the human's Christmas Day, and even though the shifters didn't celebrate the holiday, Gunnar knew there was something special about his cub. He was bigger than expected, and even the healer had advised once, "Wow, your cub will be a fighter."

Gunnar had felt pride that day. They'd gone ahead and found out the sex, because, to be honest, he couldn't wait, and neither could his mate. Although they knew, Anna Claire was to pick out the cub's name, and she did a fine job of giving their cub an honorable one.

"Your cousin would have approved of you," Gunnar said as the cub began to fuss. "You need your mama. Let's go wake her up."

Anna Claire must've heard RC fussing. A female's ability to know the sound of their cub was fascinating to him, and the care she took with him was naturally born into the shifters.

Family was everything to them, and over the summer and fall, they'd come to include the panthers in some of their gatherings. Although times were tough in the human world, and the panthers were working with the government now, a few of them would stop by occasionally to check on the lands while they were in hibernation.

Two weeks after the first of June, the sheriff had stopped by the clan to inform them a human male had finally been captured by a grizzly clan outside of Salt Lake City, Utah. He had been identified as the hacker who'd started the war against the shifters. The sheriff didn't have much information other than the threat had been taken out and the message boards had been removed. Gunnar was grateful it'd been stopped before anyone else had been killed. All the shifters ever wanted to do was live in peace.

Gunnar was thankful for the friendships they'd built with the panthers, and he was more than excited for what that meant for his clan. They'd come together because of Anna Claire, and as horrific as their first encounter had been, Gunnar was glad he had been there the day she was freed from her father and his reign. He'd taken it upon himself to heal the female, promising to love her until they found themselves in the afterlife…and then he'd love her for the rest of eternity.

Other Books by Theresa Hissong:

Fatal Cross Live!
Fatal Desires
Fatal Temptations
Fatal Seduction

Rise of the Pride:
Talon
Winter
Savage
The Birth of an Alpha
Ranger
Kye
The Healer
Dane
Booth
Noah

Morgan Clan Bears
Mating Season
Mating Instinct
Mating Fever

Incubus Tamed
Thirst

Standalone Novella
Something Wicked

Book for Charity:
Fully Loaded

Club Phoenix
The Huntress

Cycle of Sin on Tour
Rocked (A Rockstar Reverse Harem Novel)

About Theresa Hissong:

Theresa is a mother of two and the wife of a retired Air Force Master Sergeant. After seventeen years traveling the country, moving from base to base, the family has settled their roots back in Theresa's home town of Olive Branch, MS, where she enjoys her time going to concerts and camping with her family.

After almost three years of managing a retail bookstore, Theresa has gone behind the scenes to write romantic stories with flare. She enjoys spending her afternoons daydreaming of the perfect love affair and takes those ideas to paper.

Look for other exciting reads…coming very soon!

Printed in Great Britain
by Amazon